THE FOURTH POWER

A PARANORMAL WOMEN'S FICTION ROMANCE NOVEL

MICHELLE M. PILLOW

MICHELLEPILLOW.COM

ABOUT THE BOOK

Heather Harrison sees ghosts. It's not something she brags about. In fact, she wished she didn't. Communicating (or not communicating) with the dead only leads to heartache, and for her it led to a divorce. For the most part, she's happy being single. She's got a good business, close friends, and a slightly overprotective brother. What more does a forty-something woman need?

When her two best friends beg her for help in contacting loved ones, against her better judgment she can't say no to the séance. But some gateways shouldn't be opened, and some meddling spirits shouldn't be stirred...like that of her Grandma who insists she's "found her a nice man".

The supernaturals have come out to play and it's up to this amateur medium to protect herself and her friends before the danger they summoned comes to bite them in the backside.

ORDER OF MAGIC SERIES

Second Chance Magic
Third Time's A Charm
The Fourth Power
The Fifth Sense
The Sixth Spell

Visit MichellePillow.com for details!

AUTHOR UPDATES

Join the Reader Club Mailing List to stay informed about new books, sales, contests and preorders!

michellepillow.com/author-updates/

First, thank you to everyone who helped to get this book out by its scheduled release date during a challenging time in the current global landscape. I know it has been difficult to concentrate on work with so many worries. You all rock!

To my readers and their families, my heart is with all of you. I hope you are all staying safe and healthy during this global pandemic. I know it's been hard, and I thank you for your support of my books and me during this time. Your friendships do not go unnoticed.

AUTHOR NOTE

Being an author in my 40s, I am thrilled to be a part of this Paranormal Women's Fiction #PWF project. Older women kick ass. We know things. We've been there. We are worthy of our own literature category. We also have our own set of issues that we face— empty nests, widows, divorces, menopause, health concerns, etc—and these issues deserve to be addressed and embraced in fiction.

Growing older is a real part of life. Women friendships matter. Women matter. Our thoughts and feelings matter.

If you love this project as much as I do, be sure to spread the word to all your reader friends and let the vendors where you buy your books know you want to see a special category listing on their sites for 40+ heroines in Paranormal Women's Fiction and Romance.

Happy Reading!

Michelle M. Pillow

For Books in the *Order of Magic* Series

"The perfect combination of spine-tingling magic, paranormal fun, and the strength of female friendships. Michelle M. Pillow delivers an emotionally powerful, must-have read." - *K.F. Breene, Wall Street Journal, USA TODAY, and Washington Post Bestselling Author*

"Michelle M. Pillow brings us yet another hilariously touching story, this one set in the world of paranormal women's fiction, and you won't want to put it down. I know I didn't! Then again, she had me at séance." - *NY Times Bestselling Author Darynda Jones*

"When the past and the present merge...awesome author Michelle Pillow brings secrets from the grave and other things that go bump in the night into a fantastic story of second chances in the second act of life." - *Jana DeLeon, NY Times, USA TODAY, & Wall Street Journal Bestselling Author*

CHAPTER ONE
FREEWILD COVE, NORTH CAROLINA

TODAY WAS NOT A GOOD DAY.

Yesterday had not been good, nor the day before, nor the year before.

Heather Harrison's eyes had opened to a world that felt dark. People sometimes talked about having a moment when everything felt normal in the seconds between sleep and wake. She never had that. The truth was always with her. Even when she wasn't thinking about it, she felt the weight of it on her heart. It lingered in her dreams and was never more pronounced than when she was alone in her house, so she avoided going home.

Keeping busy helped.

Keeping busy was easier said than done.

"I still love you." Ben struggled with his words, and Heather struggled to look at him.

She didn't want to be here.

She didn't want to be anywhere.

The sound of silverware clinked against ceramic plates and punctuated the murmured conversation from other tables in the diner. Freewild Cove was a small town, and she felt like everyone watched their booth for the next chapter of the Harrison family story.

Heather held the coffee cup between her hands, barely feeling the heat against her fingers as she stared into the depths. Ben had insisted on ordering food, but the plates sat untouched next to them.

"Heather, I still love you, but..."

Her eyes lifted from the dark liquid. Ben looked as exhausted as she felt. Whenever she saw his face, she was reminded of all they had lost. At first, his eyes had been bloodshot all the time from crying, but the red faded until all that was left was the hollow echo of the man he'd been. There was no bringing that piece of his soul back.

She reached across the table and squeezed his hand. The warmth of human contact felt strange. His thumb slipped over her fingers to hold her hand in his.

"I still love you, but..." he whispered.

"I know." Heather pulled away. A lack of love had never been their problem. In fact, the opposite could be argued.

Ben reached beside him on the booth to lift a folder toward her. When she took it, he offered a pen from his front pocket. For them, there was no other choice. She opened the folder and signed her name beside the indicator tab, not bothering to read the papers. With that flow of ink, her marriage was over.

No, that wasn't true. Their marriage had ended over a year ago, on the day they lost their son. This was merely a formality.

"I still love you..." He tried to finish the thought, but the words kept sticking in his throat.

"But every time you look at me you see him," she answered, sliding out of the booth. "I know."

Ben nodded. She knew everything he wanted to say. They were the same words circling through her mind. Their eyes met in silence as she stood.

I'm sorry.

I miss him.

It's too painful to be here.

I will always love you.

I can't look at you.

Goodbye.

Heather nodded once, leaving the papers on the table for him to mail to the lawyers. Neither of them cared how fast the paperwork was processed, only that their part in the dealings was finished. As far as they were concerned, they were over. Together they were drowning. Maybe apart they could catch a breath.

Maybe.

Probably not.

"Oh, hey, Heather, hi." Leslie Pearson rented one of their properties. No, wait, one of *her* properties. She was no longer married.

Heather nodded once and tried to slip past the woman.

"I've been meaning to call you," Leslie continued, blocking her from leaving. "There's something up with the heater. It's making a *clunk-clunk-clang-clunk* type noise and—"

"Okay." Heather reached into her back pocket, pulled out a small notebook, and then grabbed a pen off the hostess stand. She jotted down the complaint. "I can be by tomorrow at around ten in the morning to look at it."

"Oh, great, thanks, perfect," Leslie said. "Well, wait. What time? I mean, I might have an appointment tomorrow—"

The bells over the door rang, and the diner door bumped Leslie in the shoulder as it opened.

"Sorry, excuse me." Vivien Stone had been Heather's best friend since middle school. She was everything Heather was not—bold and unflinching. She didn't wait for Leslie to answer before tugging at Heather's arm. "We're going to be late. Come on."

Heather allowed herself to be pulled out of the diner as Leslie said something about making ten work. Vivien escorted her down the sidewalk of downtown Freewild Cove at a brisk pace pausing only to avoid being hit by a car as they crossed the street.

"Where are we going?" Heather asked, confused.

Vivien led her to the front of the Warrick Theater, a building Heather had inherited from her grandmother. She stopped at the door and said, "key," before digging into Heather's front pocket to retrieve the keyring for herself. She unlocked the theater and stepped aside to let Heather go in first.

The theater was only open on weekends, and so the lights were off, and the concession stand was empty. Except for the ghost of a woman in a 1940s dress standing near the curtain leading to the theater seats, they were alone. Heather ignored the spirit.

She had nothing left to give the dead. The one spirit she wanted to see had not come to her.

When the front door closed and they were alone in the dark lobby, Vivien dropped the keys on the floor and wrapped her arms around Heather, pulling her close.

"Did your dumbass actually think I wouldn't know what you were doing today?" Vivien whispered.

Vivien had been born with psychic gifts. Not many people believed her, but Heather knew it was true. Just as Vivien believed that Heather had inherited the ability to see ghosts from her grandmother, Julia Warrick.

Her friend held her tighter. A tear slipped down Heather's cheek, and her shoulders gave an involuntary jerk as she tried to hold back a sob.

"You're not alone," Vivien said, keeping a firm grip around her. "I'm here, and I'm not leaving you. I won't let go. Ever."

Heather's legs gave out, and she felt herself lowering to the hard lobby floor. Vivien went to the ground with her, not letting go as sorrow racked Heather's body.

CHAPTER TWO
OLD ANDERSON HOUSE, FREEWILD COVE

Ten Years Later...

"Why won't you look at me? Like, I know you see me. I hate that. He never looked at me. All these hours spent working out, and he never looked..."

Heather tried to focus on what Martin Edwards was telling her about the property's old wiring and fire hazards, but it was difficult with an erratic ghost shouting in her ear for attention. The spirit's words sounded garbled like she was underwater, but even with the distortion, Heather could detect a valley girl inflection in her voice. The ghost's feathered hair and very distinct style revealed she'd most likely died in the 1980s. Heather couldn't make out everything the dead woman said, and the spirit's inclination to turn up the volume didn't do Heather's headache any favors.

Usually, if Heather concentrated hard enough, she could block them out, but this woman was persistent. All of the undead Heather had come across lately had been that way. Ever since she found her grandmother's old ring in a tax receipt box, Heather's gifts as a medium had gone into overdrive.

"Look! Just look at my perfect ass..."

The only reason she didn't throw the ring into a firepit was that her two best friends, Lorna and Vivien, had also received rings. The three of them were joined by magic. Though she'd known Vivien nearly their entire lives, Lorna was a new friend. The three of them had been brought together for a reason —to help each other heal from past pains.

Lorna was a widow. At the funeral, she'd learned her husband had another wife. The bastard had married Lorna second, and the first wife (being a spiteful bitch) had taken everything she could get her hands on. They'd séanced Glenn back so Lorna could give him a piece of her mind and find closure. She was now dating Heather's brother, William.

Vivien's case had been harder. The love of her life had died from cancer when she was in her twenties, and until recently, she'd been carrying a torch for him. Sam would not have wanted Vivien to live without love. Thankfully, with a little nudge from the afterlife, Sam was able to say a proper goodbye, and Vivien was able to give love a second chance with her new neighbor, Troy.

Heather wasn't looking for love. Her ex-husband was a good man. He'd treated her well. She had no relationship hurt to get over. Her pain ran deeper. There was no getting over the loss of a child. And even if there was some way to get over it, Heather didn't want to.

"He, like, shoved me overboard so he could be with his grody mistress..."

"So? What do you want me to do?" Martin asked, sounding a little exasperated. He was new in town, but she'd already used him on a couple of jobs. His dark hair was long enough to pull out of his face without creating a ponytail down his back. He seemed guarded but had a kindness in him. His work wasn't cheap, but it was fair.

Vivien liked to point out that he was easy on the eyes, but all Heather cared about was that his work was solid. She had a three-story Victorian to renovate, and she needed a man with solid work. Period.

"Fine, I might have fallen off the boat, but he didn't, like, try very hard to..."

Heather swatted her hand by her ear like she shooed an insect while trying to get the ghost to back away. "I'm sorry. What were my options again?"

"Hey, that's rude!"

"Patch or replace all of the wiring," Martin said.

Heather leaned against the wall to look into an opening cut in the lath and plaster. The *whoosh-pop* of a nail gun sounded in a steady rhythm, overshadowing the undertones of a radio as a couple of guys worked in the next room. She found comfort in the sounds of work. The thud of a bucket sliding across a bare floor, the thump of work boots, and even the crash of a sledgehammer felt like forward movement. It symbolized progress, momentum, the satisfaction of seeing change happen. Refurbishing houses gave her a sense of control. She could make things better.

Isn't that what mattered in life? Making things better when you could?

The ghost leaned toward the hole with her and continued talking, *"So are you going to, like, help me or what? I know you can see me."*

Heather glanced to the side.

"Ah, see, you just looked. I knew it!"

The electrical wires were old and covered in varnished cloth. They had frayed in some places. "We can't leave that in there."

"That's what I was just saying," Martin said, sounding a little annoyed.

"Look at me!"

"So you agree," Martin continued, having no clue someone else interrupted them. "We completely rewire—"

"Omigod, shut up," Heather cried, shaking her hands by her ears.

The ghost gasped but remained where she stood.

"I'm... sorry?" Martin looked stunned.

"I mean, sure." Heather rubbed her temples. She waved her hand in dismissal, needing to get away from the living so she could deal with her pest. "Do whatever you think."

"Are you pissed at me for something?" Martin asked, starting to follow her through the construction debris toward the stairs. "If you're not happy with my work—"

"Dude, stop. No, it's not you," one of the workers said in a hushed tone as he rushed to stop Martin. Thomas had worked with her many times and was one of the best drywall guys in town.

"But—" Martin tried to say.

"Leave it alone," Thomas said.

Heather pretended not to hear the conversation

as she reached the stairwell that would take her down to the second story.

"But..." Martin insisted.

"You know what today is, right?" Thomas continued.

Heather hurried down the steps and whipped around the corner so she wouldn't have to hear more. It was no surprise that everyone knew her business, but she didn't have to listen to them talk about it.

The stairs leading to the first floor were wider and led to a small landing next to a wall with a stained-glass window. From there, it split into two directions. Left would take her straight into the kitchen, and right would take her around to the front room.

In the front room, the original wood banisters were beautiful, as if they had somehow survived against the onslaught of time and people. She had always thought of their permanence compared to those who touched them.

Drop cloths covered the floors, and she glanced up from habit to check the progress of the ceiling. Someone had sprayed it with popcorn texture in the 1970s, and Heather had it removed.

Hearing someone coming down the stairs, she rushed toward the front door and down the porch steps. She'd parked in front of the house next to the curb so that she could leave whenever she wanted. Martin's truck was in the drive blocking in a car. Movement caught her eye on her way past as she stumbled to see a young face looking at her through the sun-reflected glass. Her heart nearly stopped beating. Time held still and silent in those brief seconds.

"Trav?" she whispered. The ghost of her son had never appeared to her, and yet in that instant she saw him mirrored back to her in sun and shadows.

Heather made a move toward the truck. The light shifted, and she realized it was a young girl in a baseball cap, sitting inside the vehicle, not her son. The girl staring at her through the window appeared to be around ten years old. Her lips moved, but Heather couldn't hear what she was saying.

Heather had been warned that bereaved parents sometimes see their children everywhere at first. That it was normal. She never had. She'd searched everywhere for her son, amongst every crowd, in every shadow. With all the ghosts she'd seen in her lifetime, she never saw the only one she needed.

Heather lifted her hand in greeting and forced herself to keep walking despite the heaviness in her chest. She hadn't realized Martin had a daughter.

She was a cute kid and looked a lot like her father, down to the Edwards Construction hat on her head.

"It's okay. You don't have to be scared."

Heather turned to see the girl had opened the window to shout at her.

"I'm fine. I was just startled," Heather answered.

The girl started talking to herself as she rolled up the window to continue playing.

"Finally. Are you going to help me now or what?"

Heather stiffened as her pest reappeared. She hurried toward her car, digging in the pocket of her overalls for a set of keys.

"Go away," Heather whispered. "I can't help you."

"Can't or won't?" the spirit demanded.

"Both. I can't and I won't," Heather snapped, finally managing to open her door. As she turned on her engine, she muttered, "Just go away. Not today. Just leave me alone."

"Oh, I'll leave, but you're totally going to be sorry you treated me like this."

The pain behind her eyes lessened as the ghost disappeared. The engine hummed as she sat in the car. She leaned forward to look at Old Anderson House, so named for the Anderson family that had built it in 1883 in the Queen Anne style prevalent in that period. Her favorite part was the small cupola on the top that served as a lookout toward the ocean.

A knock on her window caused her to jump a little in surprise. Martin lifted his hands to show her he hadn't meant to startle her. Heather took a deep breath before rolling down her window to apologize.

"You know, some of the guys say it's haunted," Martin said before she could get the words out.

"What?" Heather frowned in confusion and followed his gaze to the house. "Oh, yeah, no, it's not."

There was sympathy in his smile when he looked at her, and she knew he was trying to put her at ease after her mini-explosion. Little did he know her blow-up had nothing to do with him, or maybe he did but for the wrong reason. She had no idea how much Thomas had just told him.

"The guys always think the old houses we work on are haunted." She twirled the ring on her forefinger. She felt the tingling of magic in the heirloom jewelry. Except for the ghosts who occasionally followed her inside, the house had been spirit free. "I think they're disappointed when nothing supernatural happens."

Half of the big, tough men she worked with would pee themselves if they saw a real spirit.

"Well, it would make sense." Martin nodded. "A place like this has seen its share of secrets. There's a lot of history here. I feel privileged to be working on it."

She liked that about him. Martin respected the properties and their pasts. When he smiled, the look became infectious, and she found herself returning the expression.

"Maybe you should be paying me to be here, then," she joked.

"Not that privileged," he quickly amended, lifting his head to glance at his daughter in the truck. "I still need the paycheck."

"I owe you an apology." Heather's smile faded. Even though it had not been directed at him, she said, "I should never have lost my temper."

"That's all right. If anyone is going to yell at me, might as well be a pretty lady." Martin's smile went from friendly to charming.

"It's not all right but thank you for being so understanding." Heather rested her hand on the wheel, feeling the vibration of the car through her fingers.

Martin again leaned up to look at his truck.

"She's a beautiful girl," Heather said. "I didn't know you had children."

"Just the one," he said. "Jan's my little tomboy. She's always getting into some kind of mischief. She keeps me on my toes, that's for sure."

"And her mother? Is she—?"

"No, she's not."

Heather detected the shadow moving across his gaze. She knew that emotion well. "I'm sorry. When did you lose her?"

Martin's eyes widened in surprise as she guessed the truth.

"When Jan—*January*—was born. We'd been married a few years. There were complications, and I almost lost both of them. Jan's my miracle baby." He looked at his hand resting on the door. "I'm sorry. This is probably the last thing you want to be talking about right now. I only came out to make sure you were all right and to tell you I can start on the wiring first thing in the morning if you want me to."

Heather nodded. "That'll be fine. I have an inspector coming tomorrow to look at the plumbing so we can close up the walls. With the way the city has been acting about this place, I don't want them forcing me to open them back up so they can see later."

"I'll stay out of the way," he said.

"And I'm glad you told me about your wife. Jan

looks like a sweet kid, and I would hate to upset her by asking. Maybe on a different day you could introduce me properly?"

"Sure thing." Martin stood and stepped back from the car. "Have a nice day, Mrs. Harrison."

"Call me Heather," Heather corrected. "And you too."

Heather put the car into gear and drove away. The little notebook she kept in her back pocket poked her butt and reminded her of the list of things she needed to do. But as she took the winding road overlooking the coast, she found herself drawn to see her friends instead.

Hopefully Vivien and Lorna would be home. The two were roommates. Lorna worked for Heather at the historic theater she'd inherited from her grandmother, Julia Warrick. Heather knew for a fact Lorna was off today. Vivien set her own work schedule. Whether or not she would be home was anyone's guess. Since both women had boyfriends, it was possible they would have plans that didn't include a third—*or would it be fifth?*—wheel.

The ache inside Heather grew, and she didn't want to be alone. All that waited at her house was silence. Lately, that quiet had become unbearable.

Before she'd thought too deeply about what she

was doing, she found herself parked in Vivien's driveway. Her hands still gripped the wheel as the motor ran, and her foot pressed down hard on the brake. She took a shaky breath, having to will her fingers to un-pry themselves so she could take the car out of gear.

"Heather?" The window muffled Vivien's voice. She watched her friend step off of her boyfriend's front porch. Even in old cargo pants and a worn t-shirt Vivien managed to look beautiful.

Troy lifted his hand in a small wave. Heather couldn't return the gesture. She breathed deeper, each intake feeling like smoke choking her lungs.

Vivien patted Troy on the chest and said something before crossing the lawn to open the passenger side door. She slid into the seat next to her. "You should have come sooner."

Vivien met her gaze, studying her. Heather opened her mouth, but no sound came out.

Vivien nodded in understanding. They'd been friends for a long time. At first, Heather had been drawn to the fact that Vivien had also been born with psychic abilities. Whereas Heather was a medium and could see and talk to the dead, Vivien was empathic. With one look, she sensed things about people. The technical term was clairsentient because she felt what other people were feeling and understood why they might be feeling that way. She was also claircognizant because she knew if people were telling the truth. Vivien's ancestors had been carnival workers, just as Heather's grandmother had been a famous spiritualist performing on the stage.

Being that same kind of weird in middle and high school had bonded them, but it was more than that. Vivien just got her. Completely. Until they'd met Lorna, there had been no one else who Heather would have called a best friend.

Vivien slowly nodded. "I felt today was going to be a bad one. I should never have let you be alone today of all days. Not on the anniversary."

"He's gone," Heather managed, the word coming out in a harsh whisper. Pain rolled through her like a wave. Some days she could manage it. Now she could not. "I miss him so much."

Vivien wrapped her arms around Heather and pulled her tight against her. "I know, sweetie. I know. It's not fair."

Heather felt her hair lift from her head with an annoying static charge. She was too sad to care at the moment. Since they'd put on the rings, it happened whenever they touched each other. The jewelry amplified their natural abilities and also allowed them to peek inside each other's souls with one touch. It went much deeper than Vivien's empathic tendencies. Heather felt Vivien's concern as real as if it were her own. And in return, Vivien would feel Heather's heartache.

Lorna appeared in the doorway to the home she shared with Vivien and hurried down the driveway to the car. She placed her hand flat on the driver's side window. The ring on her forefinger clinked against the glass. She jerked the handle, sliding her hand across to the edge of the doorframe to throw it open.

"What's happened?" Lorna asked, concerned. "I felt pain hit me like a tidal wave."

"Bad day," Vivien answered.

Heather concentrated on drawing breath so she wouldn't pass out. It was all she could manage. If Lorna was feeling her agony from inside the house, it meant their connection was growing beyond touch.

"That was today?" Lorna frowned. She wasn't expecting a response to her question and didn't get one. She slid her arm behind Heather's back. The flow of emotions between the three of them at the contact intensified. "Viv, help me get her inside."

CHAPTER THREE

THE TINGLE REVERBERATING down her forefinger
worked its way into Heather's tired mind. She'd cried
until her mind became numb, and her sinuses were
swollen and she couldn't breathe through her nose.
Thankfully, Vivien and Lorna had not needed her to
be coherent. Some pain could not be put into words.

Lorna was a born caretaker. She'd anticipated
what Heather might need before Heather realized it
herself. Within minutes, Lorna had wrapped a
blanket around her shoulders and had handed her a
box of tissues and a mug of tea. When Heather had
exhausted her tears, Lorna helped her to Vivien's
bedroom to rest on the king-sized bed. Vivien had
laid beside her as Lorna stroked her hair.

Heather had fallen asleep surrounded by friends,

but even they could not erase the image of her son's face flashing in the truck window. That startling instant kept replaying in her mind. She'd resisted séancing Trav, and before today had only seen his face in memories and pictures.

Yes, the ceremony had worked to bring back Lorna and Vivien's dead husbands so that they both could say goodbye and let go. It wasn't a matter of if they *could* do it. It was if they *should* do it. If her son was in a better place, she did not want to drag him back to the mortal world for her own selfish reasons. There were so many unknowns to the afterlife, and she feared doing more harm than good.

But that didn't mean the ache inside her wasn't real. It was something no parent should ever have to live through. There were days she wished she'd died too.

"Don't think that," Vivien whispered sleepily from behind her. Vivien's hand rested next to Heather's back. "None of this was your fault, and your dying would only make the world a terrible place."

The mattress shifted, and she felt Vivien moving behind her. Moonlight came through the bedroom window, barely piercing the darkness. By the light she knew the moon wouldn't be very full. "Thank you for letting me stay. I couldn't go home."

"You shouldn't have tried to work. I tell you that every year." Vivien moved her hand over Heather's arm. "You should move in with us. I feel strongly that it would be good for all of us. Lorna and I would love to have you here. William can help us build another suite onto the house for you to live in." She shifted behind her only to tease. "Not that I mind spooning with you."

Heather's brother, William, worked as a contractor building houses. If she had her guess, he was currently sleeping in the other room with Lorna. The two had been dating for months. She liked Lorna with William. Her brother had never been in love, at least not like this.

It wasn't the first time that Vivien had asked her to move in. Being a social creature by nature, Vivien enjoyed having her friends around her.

"It could be fun," Vivien prompted.

"What if things progress with you and Troy? Maybe you'll want him to move in here with you," Heather countered.

"Maybe. Someday," Vivien agreed, "but that's not today. I love Troy. You know I do, but you're my best friend, my sister. Our bond goes deeper than boyfriends. If Troy loves me, he'll understand that about me. I think you should really consider moving in with us. It's not good for you to be alone. Not if you're feeling like this."

"I can't." Heather lived in the house she'd been in when her son died. Moving anywhere else felt wrong. She couldn't shake the feeling of, *what if he came home?*

"I wish I knew how to make it better for you," Vivien said. "It's not like what happened to Lorna and me. I can feel all the reasons why you don't want us to séance him back, and they are valid concerns."

Heather shook her arm to knock Vivien's hand away. She didn't want her to keep reading her emotions.

Vivien sighed. "You rarely talk about it. Maybe you should."

"You know what happened," Heather dismissed, moving to sit on the edge of the bed. Her head still ached from crying. "Talking about it doesn't change things."

"Neither does locking it up inside," Vivien countered. "Heather, you can't..."

Heather slowly stood from the bed.

"It's not..." Vivien struggled to find the right words. "It's not healthy for you to..."

Heather glanced toward the bed but couldn't see her friend beyond the faint outline of her body in the dark.

"It's not my place to tell you how to feel," Vivien said, sounding resigned. "I love you. Whatever you need. Whenever you need it. For however long."

"I know. Thank you." Heather moved toward the door. "Right now I need to go home."

"But it's in the middle of the night," Vivien protested. "Stay. I promise I'll stop pushing."

"It's not you. I have to meet the city inspector early this morning for Anderson House." Heather felt around on the floor with her feet, looking for her shoes.

"Can't that wait?" Vivien asked, not moving from the bed.

"It's already waited. It took me two weeks to get this appointment. If I miss it, I'll have to stop the remodel." Her foot bumped something, and she reached down to find her boot.

"I thought you needed inspections after the work was done." Vivien stretched her arms over her head and slid her body down on the mattress but didn't get up. She suppressed a yawn. "I still can't believe you finally own that house. They don't make them like that anymore."

"Yeah, normally the inspections come later, but the city is up my ass about it," Heather muttered. She shoved her foot into the untied boot and rocked it back and forth until it slid into place.

"That sounds fun." Vivien gave a short laugh. "Make sure they buy you dinner first."

"They have delayed construction three times already while they research my decisions on the historical property, insisting they are allowed to do that. Only to realize they'd never actually made Anderson House an official historic property, which means I have a small window to advance the work skipping some of their nonsense and delays. If I can get the inspector's okay on the plumbing job so far, we can close up some walls and prove later when the city finally gets their shit together that I did everything correctly. It's been—"

"Though I normally find talk of asses and pipe-laying fascinating, it's the middle of the night. Turn your brain off and come back to bed," Vivien said.

"Sorry," Heather responded. She liked thinking about work. It meant she wasn't thinking about other things. "You go back to sleep. I'll leave you alone."

"No, I'm sorry. Stay, at least until it's light outside." A muffled *thump-thump* sounded as if Vivien patted the bed. "You can borrow anything you want out of my closet to go meet the inspector. Maybe one of the strapless numbers to ensure you pass."

"Thanks, but I don't think Melissa is into me in that way," Heather answered.

"You never know." Vivien gave a tired laugh.

"I'm fairly certain. She's married with ten kids. I'd say she's into her husband." Heather thought of Anderson House, which made her think of Martin Edwards, which in turn made her think of being at the Victorian in a strapless dress while he worked on the wiring. A tiny shiver of anticipation worked its way over her, and she frowned. It would be too easy to let her thoughts roam to the romantic with him.

Heather physically shook her body to push away the feelings as she shoved her foot into a second boot.

"You okay?" Vivien asked.

"Yeah, go back to sleep. I promise to call you after the inspection to check in so you don't worry," Heather answered.

What in the ever-loving hell was that trip down fantasy lane all about? She could not—*would not*—be attracted to one of the guys who worked for her. Those kinds of thoughts never entered her mind.

When she closed her eyes, she saw her son's reflection fading into Jan's. She would have sworn it was her son. Was this part of the grieving process the counselors had warned her about, the mind tricking her into seeing his face where it wasn't? The few group therapy sessions she went to had parents talking about seeing their kids all the time out of the corner of their eye—movement in the house that wasn't there, another child in a crowd, a laugh at the playground that they swore belonged to their lost child.

Heather had searched, but until the truck window she had never had one of those experiences. It made her hate her gifts as a medium. She'd thought about it often—what good was talking to ghosts when she couldn't find the only one that she wanted to see?

Heather quietly left Vivien's bedroom, shutting the door behind her. She walked the dark hall toward the living room more by memory than sight.

Seeing Trav had not made things better. She'd been convinced if she could just look at him one last time, she would feel better and that somehow she would know he was all right. Though, now, she realized how stupid that thought had been. There was no getting over something like this.

Heather was so focused on her thoughts that before she realized it, she was in her car and driving home. Her purse sat on the seat next to her. She couldn't remember if she'd grabbed it or if it had been left in the car when she arrived at Vivien's. It frightened her to think that she didn't recall getting in the vehicle or driving through the quiet streets.

Coming to a stop sign, she grabbed her phone out of her purse and voice texted Vivien, "Make sure I locked your front door." She set her phone down and placed her hands on the wheel, before again grabbing it and adding, "Thanks for everything you do for me."

Seconds later the phone dinged. Vivien messaged, "*Sleeping,*" followed by, "*I love you too.*"

Whenever she'd fallen, Vivien had been there. The one thing she'd learned was that boyfriends and husbands came and went, but friends, true friends, were there forever. Before life had beaten it out of her, she used to be a romantic. She had believed in love and happily ever afters. It made her sad to think that it was one of the things she'd lost with age.

What mattered in life was family, in whatever form that may take. For Heather, of course that included her brother, William, and their obstinately hard-to-get-along-with mother. Vivien was family. So was Lorna. And Troy by extension. Counting the names on one hand made her world seem small.

Realizing she still waited at the stop sign on an

empty street, she lifted her foot from the brake and let the car roll forward. The sky had lightened with the first peek of dawn. The color shift was subtle and not enough to stir most of the population. Only one light was on in the dark houses along the street.

Heather frowned. What was she doing on this street? It wasn't the fastest way to her home.

She slowed the car as she drove past the house with the light. The curtains were open, and a small figure moved in the window. January Edwards? Was this Martin's house?

She stopped the car and put it into park. The engine ran as she stepped out to look at the window. The child seemed to be having an animated conversation with herself as she sat backward on a couch facing the window. Heather saw the back edge of the furniture along the windowsill.

The ring on her forefinger sent a vibration down her hand, a sure sign that her magic was building. Heather walked around the back of the car, trying to see if anyone else was in the living room with the girl. Jan glanced to her side, talking and laughing and nodding as if a person was next to her. There was no one, no human, no ghost.

Heather stepped onto the lawn, standing in the shadows. She wondered if that is what she'd looked like to other people when she was a kid, talking to herself. Her mother had always told people she had imaginary friends and made uncomfortable excuses for her behavior. Julia Warrick, whom Heather received her supernatural gifts from, was her grandmother on her father's side. Her mother had enjoyed the power and money that came with the Warrick name, but not what she referred to as the family embarrassment. However, having a mother, who was ashamed of her daughter's abilities as a medium, would have been better than not having known a mother at all.

Poor Jan Edwards. It must have been hard growing up without a mother, even harder still in the years to come when puberty would rear its ugly hormone-laden head.

Heather rubbed her eyes before turning her attention back to the window. Jan stared at her. Her playful conversation was over, and her expression had become serious. The girl placed her hand on the glass, fingers spread and unmoving. If there had been a ghost, Heather would have seen it. Jan probably had an imaginary friend.

Slowly, Heather lifted her hand to wave before she hurried to get off the lawn and back into her car. The last thing she needed was to explain why she was standing outside one of her electrician's houses, peeping in the windows at the crack of dawn like a crazy stalker.

What the hell was she doing?

Heather forced herself to concentrate on the road in front of her. She needed to get her shit together. Seriously. She couldn't allow the world to spin out of control. The thread she hung onto for sanity was strong, but it was only one thread and threads could be cut.

The tingling in her hand grew, and she yanked the ring from her finger and threw it on the passenger side floor. The vibration was still there, but it had lessened with the amplifier gone.

Maybe it was time to jump off this magical path. Grandma Julia's spirit had told her that the three of them were chosen to help each other heal. Lorna had been able to confront her cheating ex-husband. Forgiving him had been hard, but Lorna had done it. Vivien had been able to say goodbye to her first husband and learned that a person could have more than one soul mate in a lifetime. She was happy dating Troy.

Heather had a different kind of pain. She didn't have an ex-husband to get over. Ben was a good man. He'd been loyal, a good father, an excellent partner, and a faithful husband. Had things gone differently, Heather knew they would still be married. But things had not gone differently. He'd moved out of town years ago. Now they couldn't even speak to each other.

Heather had heard that statistically most bereaved parents ended up divorced, but that wasn't true. The real number was less than ten percent. She thought about that sometimes, wondering if there was a way they could have made it work.

The pain of a mother was much different than the pain of a lover. Children were a part of you. They grew inside your body and took a piece of your soul with them. That ache would never go away. She didn't want it to. That's all she had left, that palpable feeling of dread and sadness.

Heather pulled into her driveway. The concrete had been cracked in the corner by a tree root beneath the ground so the car bounced as the tire rolled over it. The gray paint wasn't a color she'd pick, and it would have taken any one of the crews she used a day to knock out a new look, but she didn't have the heart to change anything. The attached garage was small and filled with construction supplies so she never parked her car in it.

MICHELLE M. PILLOW

The plan had been to do a quick remodel and sell the home for a bigger place.

The plan had been to fill that bigger place with more children.

The plan had been...

It didn't matter.

Heather got out of the car and pushed the door with her hip as she looked for her house key on the keyring. Exhaustion weighed heavily on her shoulders.

Once inside, she called out softly, "I'm home."

Silence answered her, as it always did. She didn't bother turning on lights as she moved from the living room to the kitchen. Compared to Vivien's, her home was small—three bedrooms, a living room, a kitchen, and a bathroom. The master bedroom wasn't a suite, and one of the bedrooms was her office. There was extra space in the half-finished basement.

At the end of the hall were three doors—to the right was her office, in the middle was the bathroom, and to the left was her son's room. She touched the door lightly as she moved past it into the bathroom. A tiny smudge of old adhesive had been left over from a truck sticker, but her fingers no longer stuck to it when she touched it. In the beginning, she used to go inside every day and look for him, but she never went into Trav's bedroom anymore.

Heather stood in the bathroom for a long time, staring at her face in the mirror until the blurring of her eyes caused her features to distort and become unrecognizable. She stopped seeing herself and instead became haunted by the flash of her son's face in the reflected truck window. It wasn't like staring at a photograph hanging on her living room wall or watching a video. He'd moved freely as if he'd been sitting in the vehicle.

No. She couldn't let herself become deluded. It was a trick of the mind. Jan had been sitting in the truck.

Determined to start her day as she did any other, she turned on the shower and undressed. There was plenty that needed to be done, and if she worked her way down that list, she would know what to do with her time. The hours would be filled, and she wouldn't have to stop and think.

CHAPTER FOUR

WARRICK THEATER FELT MORE like a childhood home than her mother's house. Heather had spent hours as a child running along the aisles, watching old movies, and hiding in the apartment upstairs. The building was over a hundred years old, and according to the plaque the city had placed on the front of the building, it had been commissioned by local businesswoman and suspected witch Julia Warrick. Some called Heather's grandmother a witch, and maybe she had been, but Julia had identified as a spiritualist and a medium. She had held séances in the theater, and clients would travel hundreds of miles to speak to their loved ones through her.

Nowadays, though, the business was what one

would expect from a historical theater—movies and stage performances. They even managed to book a few indie film auditions.

"Grandma?" Heather called into the empty building. She felt tiny strands of hair tickling her face and tried smoothing them into the bun at the nape of her neck. Luckily meeting a housing inspector at a job site in work clothes wasn't frowned upon and didn't require anything fancy. "Are you here?"

The spirit didn't show herself.

Heather and William had inherited the building, but her brother had sold his half to her. At the time, he didn't believe in ghosts and thought, much like their mother, that Julia was a con woman. He knew better now. Seeing was believing.

Heather moved past the concession stand in the front lobby toward the curtain hanging over the theater doorway. Julia often manifested near the seats. The Warrick Theater was a small venue compared to the multiplexes. They only had a hundred and four cushioned seats.

Heather told people she wanted to modernize the décor but couldn't because of the building's historical status. But, in truth she didn't push too hard. The gold and burgundy sponge-painted walls, art deco light fixtures, and paneled ceiling might be out of fashion, yet they reminded her of Julia, and of her childhood. This theater was one of the few places she had felt normal as a kid.

When she'd hired Lorna to manage the place, Heather hadn't expected things to turn out the way they did. Lorna was the best theater manager she'd ever hired. Within a short period of time, she'd had the place booked solid. Sure, they had to cancel some of the shows because Heather, Lorna, and Vivien accidentally summoned a demon to terrorize the theater, which in turn attacked Lorna and put her in the hospital. But they'd taken care of that, and the theater was getting back on schedule.

"Grandma?" Heather called as she walked down the aisle toward the stage. "Are you here?"

"Here, there, nowhere," Julia's voice answered, but the ghost did not appear.

Crap.

Heather recognized the tone. When Julia manifested it could be from any part of her timeline. Younger Julia, who'd lived in the 1920s, was one of the more challenging to get answers from. It wasn't surprising since Julia, as a bootlegger and marijuana grower, had trust issues.

"Grandma, can you show yourself, please?"

"You know I hate it when you call me that."

Julia's transparent body appeared in a seat. The muffled sound of her voice felt far away.

Heather reached for her hand. She'd flung the ring off that morning in a fit, and it was now somewhere on the floor of her car. When the ring amplified her abilities, it had also made the ghosts easier to hear.

Julia's leg draped over the arm of her seat, and she swung her foot lightly as if bored. She wore high-waisted trousers and a matching vest over a dress shirt. There was no denying her grandmother had been glamorous during that era. Her short hair had finger waves, and she looked like she belonged in a Gatsby movie.

"But you are my grandma," Heather reasoned, hoping a sentimental thread would trigger an older version of Julia.

"Can't you call me by my name?" Julia asked.

Heather felt like she had cotton shoved in her ears, muffling the words.

"Grandma makes me sound *old*," the spirit complained.

"Okay, Julia," Heather said, playing along. "I need your help."

"What is it, doll?" Julia lifted her fingers, and a cigarette appeared between them. Smoke curled from the tip before disappearing. Most of the time, like now, Heather couldn't smell the phantom smoke.

Usually ghosts were stuck in one moment of their lives. Those residual hauntings didn't even know they were dead as they lived moments over and over. Julia was an intelligent haunting, aware of her surroundings. No, she was more than that, she was a *super*-intelligent haunting. She changed her age and style like the living picked outfits, was aware of her death (not all intelligent hauntings were), and could communicate better than most.

"Are you finally ready to ask about your love life?" Julia asked, appearing put out by the thought. "Do you know how many women come to me for that? I bet it's the same for you. I say I can talk to the dead, and when they get their chance to ask a question it's always about a man. Does he love me? Will I meet him? Where is he? Will we be married? Is he handsome?"

Heather opened her mouth to interrupt, but Julia held up a hand and shook her head to stop her.

"Handsome? Can you believe it? That's what they always care about. Rich and handsome. I think twice in all my life did a woman ask me if he was kind first, instead of like an afterthought. There is beauty in kindness, and in the right heart. That's all that matters really at the end of things, and in the middle for that matter. A handsome face only matters in the beginning. Who plans a story for its beginning, though? I used to tell them to forget about tall, dark, and handsome and focus on themselves. You can imagine how well that answer goes over half the time. They pretend to nod, but it's all—"

"Julia, I'm not looking for handsome," Heather interrupted.

"Too bad, cause you're getting it. He's smart too, and kind." Julia laughed. "With a body like a Greek—"

"I'm not asking about my love life," Heather broke in.

"You should." Julia lowered her voice. It was hard enough hearing what she said in her normal tone that the decreased volume forced Heather to lean toward her. A tiny ache started in her temple as she focused on Julia's words. "Your kitty cat isn't growing any younger, but the right man can make it purr."

Heather shot up and back, pulling away. "Ew, Grandma, come on. I don't want to talk about my dating life."

"Even if I've located a nice man for you?"

"Yes, even if," Heather dismissed. "I need you to be serious for a moment."

"Well, out with it," Julia urged. "It's not like I have an eternity to—actually." She laughed. "I do have an eternity."

"Have you seen my son?" Heather could barely get the words out.

The cigarette disappeared from her fingers, and Julia's features aged by small degrees. Her hairstyle changed but was still shorter. She slid her leg from the arm of the chair and made a move to stand before disappearing. Seconds later, she reappeared in the aisle between Heather and the stage. A long green dress with small yellow flowers had replaced her pantsuit. Her face had aged a few decades.

"I haven't seen him." Julia reached her hand forward as if to touch Heather's cheek. Heather felt a slight chill at the touch but nothing substantial. "Did you see him? Do you have reason to believe he's here?"

"I thought I did, but..." Heather rubbed her temple. The ache in her head was growing stronger the longer they spoke. She should have never taken off the ring. "Can you look for him? On your side? Is that possible?"

If anyone could find him, it was her grandmother.

Julia closed her eyes and slowly shook her head. "I don't sense him. If you want to look for him, you know what you have to do."

Julia's words were becoming harder to hear. Heather nodded. "My mind was playing tricks on me, I guess. I thought I saw him in a reflection, but it doesn't make sense that he would come now."

"Maybe your magic was trying to tell you something important, and that was its way of getting your attention." Julia's spirit faded, and her voice softened. "You should..."

"Grandma?" Heather turned in a circle, searching for the spirit, but she was gone. "I should what?"

Should séance her son?

No. Heather didn't want that for him. Séancing him would be a purely selfish act unless she had reason to believe he wasn't at rest. Trav had been such a good boy. There was no reason for him to be sticking around.

"Grandma?" she called, willing the ghost back. "Julia?"

She received no answer. Why had she taken off the damned ring?

Heather rushed through the theater and out the front door. She ran to her car and fumbled with the passenger door lock. Once inside, she searched the floor for her ring, running her hand under the seat and along the edge. Her fingertips hit metal. She worked and stretched her fingers, trying to knock the ring closer so she could grab it. Unfortunately, it rolled away from her.

"Dammit," Heather swore. "Come here!"

She felt something moving against her hand, and she jerked it from under the seat. The ring was back on her forefinger.

Heather stared at it for a moment before hurrying back inside. She ran into the theater, hoping the ring would amplify her powers and bring Julia back.

"Grandma?" she yelled. "I should do what?"

She searched the seating area and along the front of the small stage.

"Julia? What should I do?"

Heather went up the stairs along the side. The movie screen was retracted up toward the ceiling. She was able to freely search the narrow space of the back area.

"Heather?" Lorna's voice came from the theater. She sounded worried. "Heather, are you in here?"

Heather came from behind a post and onto center stage.

"Omigod, are you all right? I saw your car door standing open and thought maybe something had happened to you." Lorna did not slow her steps as she joined her on the stage. She wore a button-down shirt and jeans, and her red-highlighted brown hair was pulled back away from her face. She was dressed for work.

Heather hadn't realized she'd left the car door open.

"I was talking to Grandma Julia," Heather said, not bothering to explain how she'd searched for her ring. "She disappeared on me, and I was trying to find her again."

Even though Lorna could not see ghosts without first summoning them with Vivien and Heather, she still automatically looked around the theater from the edge of the stage. "Do you want me to call Viv and have her join us?"

Yes.

No.

Heather frowned. "Uh—"

"I'll get Viv," Lorna decided.

"—no," Heather said at the same time.

"No?" Lorna again looked around at the theater's empty seats. "Are you sure?"

No.

Yes.

Dammit.

"Yeah, I'm sure. You have to get ready for the show tonight." Heather came down the stage steps and moved up the aisle. She paused halfway up and turned around to study Lorna. "Are you doing all right here on your own?"

"Oh, yeah, sure," Lorna's answer seemed hesitant. Heather couldn't blame her since she'd been attacked by a demon while living in the apartment upstairs. It's why she'd moved in with Vivien. "It helps not spending the night. And the smudging helped—*helps*. I don't feel scared when I'm here alone during the day, creeped out a little maybe, but not frightened like before. Then the customers come, and it's not so bad. I get my work done while they're entertained and then leave soon after. Plus, your brother comes by to check on me."

"I noticed that." Heather smiled as she led the way toward the front lobby. "Things are still going well with you two?"

"Very." Lorna almost looked dreamy-eyed. "We're talking about him meeting my children soon.

I've told them all about you and Vivien. They know I've been dating, but William and I are serious, and it is probably time they all met. I don't know how they'll react. I don't expect that it will be easy to see me with someone who isn't their father."

"You deserve happiness," Heather stated.

"I know." Lorna nodded. "But so do you."

Heather didn't ask what Lorna meant by that. The comment felt like more than a general statement between friends. It turned out she didn't have to ask.

"Vivien mentioned she sensed something about you," Lorna said.

Heather suppressed a sigh as she looked out the front doors to her car. The door was closed. Freewild Cove didn't have a lot of crime, but there were petty thefts. Leaving her car door open had been stupid.

"She didn't think we should mention it, but I disagree. She said she saw a new man in your life and—"

"Not you too," Heather groaned.

"Me too what?"

"All I need is a nice guy?" Heather asked, arching a brow.

"Beats a crappy one," Lorna countered.

"My mother has been trying to set me up with the sons of her friends. I'm about to create a fake boyfriend to shut her up, like some bad rom-com plot. Julia has a nice guy picked out for me from beyond the grave. And now you and Viv, too?" Heather fought the urge to scream. Why was it whenever a woman of a certain age was single, people wanted to set them up with a man? It was an almost desperate psychological need within society to sort people into pairs. Yes, when it came to relationships, Heather was alone. But she wasn't lonely. Why couldn't people get that?

Heather felt a hand on her arm and looked down in surprise as Lorna touched her. She was thankful that her hair was pulled back, otherwise it would have been lifting off her shoulders. "I'm sorry. I didn't realize it frustrated you so much."

"I'm not..." Heather pulled her arm from Lorna's grasp. There was no point in lying. Lorna had read her emotions.

"Vivien was right. I shouldn't have said anything to you," Lorna said. "I just want you to be as happy as I am."

"I know." Heather lightly patted Lorna's shoulder. "I feel that your heart is in the right place. I'm just not in a headspace to think about relationships right now."

"Then we won't talk about them," Lorna said.

"Besides, I have something much more interesting I need to discuss with you."

"Oh?"

"Hot dog orders," Lorna stated with mock seriousness. "Do you want pork, or do we go wild and try beef?"

"Pork," Heather answered with a small laugh, appreciating Lorna changing the subject. "I like the easy questions."

"How did your inspection go at the house today?" Lorna asked.

"Melissa postponed until this afternoon. I'm about to head over there." Heather rubbed her hand, feeling the tiny vibrations from the ring.

"You go. I have everything handled here. I'm going to order supplies and do some cleaning before people show up for the movie tonight." Lorna took a step toward the back office.

Heather couldn't help but feel bad leaving Lorna alone in the theater. "Maybe I should hire another person to help you out."

"What you mean to say is, you're still worried about me being here alone so you're going to waste money on a pretense to make me feel better," Lorna corrected. "Thank you, but I promise I'm all right."

"Call me if that changes," Heather said.

"Will do. Now go. Handle your business." Lorna waved her hand toward the front doors. "And I want a tour of this Old Anderson House I've heard so much about."

"Anytime." Heather pushed open the front door and stepped out into the sunlight. Her conversation with Julia had proven to be unhelpful. She didn't have any more answers than when she'd woken up that morning.

Exhaustion was setting in. She contemplated walking down the block and around the corner to the coffee shop, but that seemed like it would take too much effort. Instead, she got into her car to drive the short distance with the excuse she'd pick up pastries for the guys. Nothing like food to provide a little extra goodwill and motivation.

CHAPTER FIVE

CHOCOLATE MUFFINS for breakfast might not have been her brightest plan.

Heather lightly pushed at her sore stomach, trying not to be obvious in her discomfort as she watched Melissa make notations on her clipboard. It was impossible to tell how the inspection was going. Melissa gave very little away with her expressions, and her handwriting was awful. Trying to covertly read her notations over her shoulder was near impossible.

"We're replacing all the wiring next," Heather said.

Melissa glanced up and nodded. Out of all the inspectors Heather had worked with over the years, she respected Melissa's no-nonsense approach to her job. She took it seriously but was always fair and worked to find solutions when there were problems.

"I found some reclaimed tiles online to repair the bathroom floor," Heather continued. The sound of footsteps ran across the ceiling. She glanced up. "Sorry, they're noisy today."

"Uh-huh," Melissa answered, appearing like she was only half-listening.

"Have I tried to bribe you with chocolate muffins yet?" Heather asked.

"Yes." Melissa smiled when she glanced up this time.

"Did it work?"

"As far as the plumbing goes, you're good to go." Melissa tore off a piece of paper from her stack and handed the duplicate page to Heather. "Keep that for your city paperwork."

"Thank you." Heather folded the paper and stuck it in her back pocket. "Seriously, that's a huge relief."

"Don't thank me yet. I've noted quite a bit of things you'll want to address." Melissa pulled another page from her stack and handed it to Heather. "I won't put this in an official report since we're not here for that yet, but I will look for these things the next time."

"Understood." Heather kept that list in her hand as she walked Melissa to the door. The sound of footsteps pounded upstairs again, and she automatically glanced upward. Who was running around on the job like that?

"You shouldn't have kids running around in here," Melissa said. "It's too dangerous."

"Kids?"

Melissa pointed up. "That sounds just like my kids playing. I had to carpet my second story just to muffle the noise."

"It does, doesn't it?" Heather frowned. Even though several of the guys had children, there shouldn't have been any running around on the job site. "I'll take care of it."

"I'll send you my bill," Melissa said, heading for the door.

Heather thanked the woman before hurrying up the stairs. Several thuds sounded and then more running. The second story consisted of four bedrooms, two on each side of the wide landing that served as a hallway between them, and a shared bathroom that was a straight shot from the stairs. If she turned around, she'd see a door next to the first floor staircase that would take her to the third story.

The sound of laughter came from one of the bedrooms. She went to the door to look inside. No one was there.

A strange sensation prickled her spine. It was difficult to explain, but it was a feeling that came over her whenever a darker spirit was present. Darker didn't always mean evil. Sometimes it meant the spirit was upset or carrying an emotional burden, which could make them dangerous if they decided to lash out, or annoying if they decided to glom onto her energy.

She glanced at her grandmother's ring and frowned. Why was a needy ghost showing up at Old Anderson House now? There was a theory that renovations sometimes stirred spirits. The idea was they didn't like their environments disturbed. Though she'd seen some evidence of it, she always attributed it to the ghosts using the workers' energy to manifest. A bunch of strong, hard-working men had to look like a supernatural buffet to some spirits.

The sounds of work came from the third floor. She heard the unmistakable rhythm of the nail gun. The faint sound of Johnny Cash singing about his heart came from a radio. That meant it was most likely Thomas. He had a thing for older country.

Footsteps came from the room across the hall. Heather went to that door to check. Aside from a stack of drywall and a few buckets, it was empty. The energy wasn't as strong in the second bedroom, but she still felt lingering traces of it.

As a mother, the idea of children's spirits being trapped in the house saddened her. It would account for the lighter footsteps.

Heather went into the open area between rooms and waited. The running sounded in a third bedroom. She didn't go to the door as she watched to see if anyone would come across. If Melissa had heard the play, that meant the guys would as well. It was only a matter of time. The last thing she wanted was to lose half her crew to otherworldly fear and to have to deal with the rumors that Old Anderson House was haunted.

To most people, rumors of a haunting would be a laughable anecdote to tell friends. For a Warrick, it was another coal on the ever-burning gossip fire.

A soft giggle came from one of the rooms, but she couldn't be sure which.

"Is someone in here?" she asked softly.

"You're it!"

Heather nearly jumped out of her skin as a figure jumped from one of the bedrooms. She inhaled sharply and stumbled back, only to catch herself before falling down the stairs. Her heart hammered violently.

When her eyes focused, Heather saw Jan staring at her with a worried expression. The child stood with her hands frozen at her sides. She wore a long-sleeve t-shirt splattered with red paint and a pair of cargo pants. After a moment, she lowered her arms.

"There's no reason to be afraid," Jan said.

"You startled me." Heather tried to force a light laugh to put the child at ease. "Is your dad around?"

"January?" Martin called as he came down the steps.

"She's down here," Heather answered.

He emerged from the stairwell. "I told you, no playing while on the job site. You're supposed to be doing homework in the tower."

"That nail gun was too loud," Jan answered.

"Since when?" Martin shook his head at his daughter before turning to Heather. "I'm sorry if she was causing trouble. I told her to stay in the cupola while the inspector was here."

"No trouble," Heather said. Realizing she still

held the list of issues Melissa had given her, she shoved the paper into her pocket for later.

"You, math, now," Martin ordered. "Don't make me tell you again."

Jan hardly looked scared. "Me, math, done. I sent it in already."

"Social Studies?"

"We won the war."

"Which war?"

Jan crossed her arms over her chest and leaned to the side in a sassy pose. "The big war."

"English?"

"Done."

Martin sighed. "English?"

"What?"

"*English?*"

Jan dropped her arms and matter-of-factly stated, "Dad, the book is stupid."

"But you're not stupid, so I know you can read the book and write that report." Martin gestured his hand toward the stairs, silently ordering her to go up.

Heather watched the interplay in silence, feeling very much like an interloper in the private conversation. Martin was clearly not just a handsome face. Somehow seeing him as an involved father only made him all that more attractive. When father and daughter looked at each other, she easily recognized the love beneath the thin layer of parental frustration and young girl rebellion.

"Negotiation," Jan demanded.

"Ice cream," Martin stated.

"And pizza," Jan countered, "with my choice of toppings."

"No candy toppings on the pizza and finish the paper first."

"And I get a dog," she added.

"Not a chance. It's not fair for him to be alone in the house all day."

"I want to use the nail gun."

"Not while I'm on a job."

"Then I want two scoops."

"B grade or higher on that report, and I'll take you for three."

"Fine. Deal"

"Fine."

Jan made a show of stomping as she went up the stairs, supposedly to do her homework.

"Don't bother Thomas," Martin called after her.

Heather listened to Jan's footsteps. The child was precocious. Martin definitely had his hands full.

He ran his hands through his hair and sighed. "Is this a problem? I promise I'll keep her out of the way.

She's enrolled in an online school. My sister was staying with us to help out, but she flaked on me. I don't have anywhere else to leave her."

"Online schools. What a strange world we live in. We didn't even get a computer in school until I was in eighth grade, and it had a giant green monitor." Heather gave a small laugh. "As long as she stays out of the dangerous areas, I don't care if she comes to work with you. I imagine it's challenging to be a single parent."

"Thank you. I appreciate that." He looked like he wanted to say more, but he turned to go upstairs.

Heather followed him as far as the bottom of the stairwell. A pair of work gloves was shoved into his back pocket. The image drew her eyes to his firm backside, and she found herself trying to stop him from leaving. "Can I ask, why is she in an online school? It seems like it might be easier just to let her go to the public one."

He stopped halfway up only to come back down. "Jan does better this way. She's an imaginative kid. Teachers haven't always appreciated that about her."

Heather was instantly sorry for the question. She could sense she touched upon a sore subject. No parent liked to feel like they were being judged for their choices. "I didn't mean for that to sound like I was criticizing the choice to homeschool. You'd know what is best for her, of course."

He again looked like he wanted to speak only to stop himself.

"I'm sure she learns a lot coming to work with you," Heather said. "I think it's great children have more options for school these days."

"It is, and she does. She likes working on the houses and asking questions, but I promise I won't let her interrupt the work or cost you any money." Martin glanced up the stairs and then back at her. "I was worried she would miss out on socializing with other kids, but..."

Heather waited for him to finish. When he didn't, she prompted, "But?"

"She doesn't," he finished flatly, as he pulled the work gloves from his back pocket and held them in a fist.

"Is there something on your mind?" Heather inched closer to him and lowered her voice. "If I offended you, or if you're worried about something, please say. I don't want you to feel tense around here. There is a ton of work to do, and I have other jobs that I'd like to hire you for."

"Yes, but no." Martin still hesitated.

"If this is about my yelling yesterday, I am truly sorry. That wasn't fair."

"I'm not sure it's my place to say anything, but I wanted to tell you that I'm sorry for your loss," Martin said.

Heather pressed her lips together and nodded, unable to meet his eyes.

"I can't imagine what you must be feeling. I promise I'll never mention it again," Martin assured her. "I'm sure the last thing you wanted was for me to bring it up."

"There are so many, many bad parts to it." Heather didn't know what made her confess her feelings. She wasn't used to opening up, and the words were never articulate when she tried. Normally, she would take the awkward condolences and get out of the conversation as quickly as possible. "I think one of the bad parts is when people know what happened, and they start trying to avoid talking about anything that has to do with kids, or babies, or motherhood, like that reminder will be what makes me remember what happened. And when they slip, you can see the panic on their faces and the apology half-formed on their lips. They mean well, but it gives it an air of shame like it's something people aren't meant to say outside of a grief therapy group."

Martin nodded, not answering. She didn't expect him to. What could he say?

"I guess what I'm trying to say is, you don't have to avoid the topic. I don't want it to be every conversation, but..."

"I think I understand." He placed a hand on her shoulder and gave her a light squeeze. The heat of his touch radiated down her arm, filling her with awareness—awareness of his touch, of how close he stood, of the heat coming through his t-shirt, of the inappropriateness of having this kind of response to someone who worked for her. It had been a long time since she'd allowed a man to touch her, or at least in a way that made her sexually interested.

Heather stepped back and dropped her shoulder. He let go.

"What happened to your son?" he asked.

Heather's mind instantly flashed back to that day.

"You don't have to answer," he said, "but I'm here if you ever want to talk about it."

"Trav was ten," she said, trying to decide how much to say, but once the words started, they didn't stop. "Ben and I decided he was old enough to ride his bike back and forth to school. For the first week, everything was fine. Then, halfway through the following week he didn't come home. People say they know agony, but that feeling when your child is missing? There's nothing that compares to it."

Martin stood quietly, listening.

"We checked the route that we'd told him to take. Then we checked the neighborhood. Then we called the school. Then we called his friends. Every minute felt like torture."

This was a pain that time did not lessen. At best, she merely learned to live with it. She swiped a tear as it tried to fall.

"The thoughts that ran through my mind that first night he was missing were awful. What if he had been kidnaped? What if some pervert had him? What if, what if...?" She again swiped her eyes and shook her head. "The next day they found him in a ditch on the side of the highway, his bike mangled. There was no reason he should have been out that far. Some of his friends dared him to take a new route home. My son had so much adventure and life in him. He was the kid that tried climbing to the top of the monkey bars at the park, only to fall, and then get right back up and try again. Completely fearless. He would have loved the challenge of taking a new route home. I feel like I should have been able to predict he might try it."

"Did they find out what happened?" Martin asked.

Heather took a deep breath. "A drunk tourist struck him with a rental and then ran from the scene. He had six drunk driving priors on his record and his license had already been suspended. His wife rented the car for him. He was charged with an aggravated felony and will get out of prison in about three years from now. They gave him the max sentence."

Martin hesitated before giving her a hug. The warmth of his arms surrounded her as he drew her against the strength of his chest. She fought her tears as the comfort of human contact surrounded her.

"I'm sorry you lost your boy," he whispered as he stroked her back.

All she could do was answer him with a nod.

She had no idea how long he held her. A loud bang sounded upstairs as something dropped. The murmur of voices from the first story workers came from below.

Not wanting to be caught in such a position by the men she'd hired, she pushed at his chest.

Martin released her from his embrace.

"I'm sorry. This isn't..." Heather stopped short of saying it wasn't appropriate for them to be holding each other on the job site. "Thank you for listening."

Martin seemed to come to the same conclusion. "I should probably get back to work. I don't get paid until the job is done."

Another bang sounded from above.

His kind smile reached into his eyes, and he nodded once.

Heather watched as he disappeared upstairs, again noting the view of him walking away. It wasn't something she'd act on. The man had sex appeal, yes, but he also had responsibilities. When you dated a single parent, you had to take into consideration there wasn't just one person in the picture.

Dating? Why was she thinking about dating? She didn't date. She didn't even have one night stands... unless her silicone boyfriend counted. She had been so busy lately that they were barely on speaking terms. He'd been abandoned in her nightstand for months.

"Stop it," Heather muttered under her breath, scolding herself. "Don't go there."

She went to the empty bedroom that Jan had jumped out from to scare her. The temperature felt colder than the rest of the house.

"Is someone in here?" Heather asked the supposedly empty room. There might not be humans, but signs pointed to a supernatural presence. The drop in temperature could indicate a sign of paranormal activity. It was one of the reasons Heather was so fond of wearing flannels during the day as part of her work clothes.

Seeing a series of tic-tac-toe games drawn in a layer of construction dust, Heather crossed the room and crouched down by an unfinished round. Had Jan been playing by herself?

She drew an X in the dust and stood. Slowly, a circle formed on the game piece as if traced with a small, invisible finger. Whoever played the game didn't show themselves.

"Who's there?" Heather asked. The circle stopped before it was completed.

She remembered what Jan kept telling her, *"You don't have to be afraid."*

Heather glanced around the room before leaning over to draw another X to let the other player easily win. She waited, but no one finished the game.

Heather went upstairs. Martin had started cutting holes in one of the walls to feed new wiring through. In another room, Thomas applied sheetrock mud along the seams of the drywall he'd just hung.

Jan was nowhere to be seen. There was only one place more to look—up the narrow circular steps to the cupola on the top of the house that looked out over the ocean.

Jan had built herself a nest with a jacket and bookbag on the floor. Her back pressed into the wood side as she stared at an e-reader.

"Hi," Heather said.

"Hey." Jan didn't look up, but her tone said she'd known Heather was there.

"You found my favorite room in the house," Heather said.

"It's cool." Jan pushed her finger on the screen, causing it to flicker.

"I always hated reading in school, too," Heather said, trying to make conversation.

"That's not true," Jan answered. "You liked the girl detective books."

Heather didn't take her eyes off the child. How could she possibly have known that unless she was gifted? "I guess I should have said I hated assigned reading."

Jan shrugged.

"Who told you I like detective books?" Heather asked.

At that, Jan finally glanced up. She shrugged again and said, "No one. I just guessed."

"Do you guess things about people often?"

Heather wondered if maybe the girl was claircognizant like Vivien.

"I don't know. Maybe sometimes." Jan didn't appear too interested in explaining. "I have to read this now."

"Yes, of course. Sorry." Heather started to leave, but something told her to stay. "You know, if you ever wanted to talk about how you know things, I'm a great listener. My friends and I, we're kind of special like that. We know things too, things that other people don't know."

"I'm not supposed to talk about it." Jan looked more thoroughly at her.

"I understand." Heather began to reach out toward her, but Jan leaned away. Heather lifted her hand and retreated from the attempt at affection. "I wasn't supposed to talk about it either. Most people never believed me when I told them I was special."

"If I don't finish this book, I don't get pizza." Jan made a point of turning her attention to the e-reader. She looked so small and young, but there was something familiar in the way she carried herself. Her eyes were sharp as if she knew secrets she shouldn't.

Something deep inside Heather told her she was supposed to help this girl.

She pulled the small notepad from her back

pocket and patted her hair to find the pen she usually stuck there. Heather wrote down her phone number and set it on the ground close to Jan. "If you ever want to talk..."

Jan glanced but didn't take the paper.

"It was nice talking to you, Jan." Heather already felt like she'd overstayed her welcome. She backed down the stairs, leaving the girl alone.

"Is everything all right?" Martin asked when she emerged from the narrow stairwell.

Heather glanced up to see Jan leaning over the side to stare down at them.

"Just girl talk." Heather smiled up at the girl and winked. She stepped out of view. "She seems like a lovely girl."

"Thanks. She is." Martin moved to return to work.

"Call me if you need anything," Heather said. "I'm going to check in at a couple of other job sites."

"Will do, boss," he answered with a small wave before plugging in an electric saw.

Heather moved slowly through the house, looking for a sign of ghosts. When she reached her car, she dialed Vivien. It didn't take long for her friend to answer.

"I was just thinking about you," Vivien said by way of a greeting.

"All good things I hope," Heather said. It was always comforting to hear her familiar voice.

"What fun would that be?" Vivien countered. "How did the inspection go?"

"Fine. She signed off on the plumbing," Heather said. "But I'm calling for another reason. I think Anderson House might be haunted. I need you and Lorna to come over here with me. Soon."

"I thought you always said that house was sans spirits," Vivien said in surprise. "You said, it was silly that people always thought old buildings were haunted just because they were old."

"I know what I said. Something unexpected happened today. I promise I'll tell you all about it later." Heather put her keys into the ignition. "Just say you'll help me."

Her phone beeped, indicating she was receiving another call.

"I'll help you," Vivien agreed. "Whatever you need."

"Thanks. I have to go." She glanced at her phone. "My mother is calling."

"Tell Bonnie I said hi," Vivien said.

"Will do." Heather tapped the phone screen,

ending one call and answering the other. "Hey, Mom."

"Heather? It's me. Mom."

"Hey Mom," she repeated, bracing herself for whatever drama was about to filter through the phone. After a lifetime, it was easy to hear the subtle nuances of Bonnie's moods in her voice. She always found it ironic that her mother's maiden name was Stable when that's not a word she'd use to describe the uptight woman. "What's up?"

"Did you know that Robert was in prison? Tell me you didn't know Robert was in prison," Bonnie demanded. "I heard them talking about it." Her voice lowered to a rushed whisper. "They were discussing prisoner relations in the shower. You know, when they drop the soap."

Robert?

"Uh, no, I didn't," Heather stated. Who the hell was Robert?

"Tell me you didn't send convicts over to my house like some kind of chain gang," Bonnie insisted.

"I didn't send convicts to your house like some kind of chain gang," Heather stated, putting the phone on speaker before driving away from Old Anderson House. "I don't think they have chain gangs anymore, Mom."

"I looked. They have prisoner ink," Bonnie stated.

My mother, the detective, Heather thought wryly. She did not let the sarcasm into her voice. "What do you know about prison ink?"

"There was a special on television last week. Did you know they melt plastic and inject it into the skin? Sometimes they mix soot with shampoo."

"Fascinating," Heather drawled. "Are you opening a tattoo parlor?"

"What? No. Who told you that?" Bonnie asked.

"Robert and his biker gang. Isn't that why you called? You're going to let them use your home as a new clubhouse?" Heather knew she was going to pay dearly for trying to tease her mother, but the words just slipped out. This was probably cosmic proof as to why William was Bonnie's favorite child.

"You're not funny."

Heather waited, knowing that wasn't the end of the lecture.

"Don't you do background checks on the people you hire? Your brother would never be this irresponsible. This is the problem with believing you can *feel* things about people. Your grandmother was the same way, always making careless decisions that affect other people. You have to start thinking, Heather.

You can't just flounce through life on a whim," Bonnie insisted.

"Mom, I—" Heather didn't flounce through anything.

"Or did you go out of your way to send a biker gang lawn service over to my house? Did you think it was funny? What did I ever do to you to deserve...?"

Her mother kept talking, but Heather stopped listening. Lawn service? This was about the people she'd sent over to mow her mother's grass?

"...thirty-six hours of labor..."

Heather automatically turned toward her mother's house. On the off chance Bonnie was talking about someone Heather had not sent over, she wanted to make sure her mother was safe. On the more likely chance Bonnie did mean the lawn people Heather had hired, she needed to act like a buffer to make sure the entire crew didn't quit on her.

"...ungrateful..."

Robert from prison? Who the hell was Robert?

"Mom," Heather interrupted, "do you mean Bobby?"

"Haven't you been listening? Where are you?"

"I'm in my car turning onto your street," Heather said.

Her childhood home was in an affluent neighborhood of Freewild Cove. The Warrick money had afforded the kind of lifestyle her mother had wanted. Large and lacking character, Heather had never really been a fan of the perfection her mother strove to achieve.

"I don't see you," her mother said, the tone mildly accusing.

Yeah, like I have nothing better to do than lie to you about coming over.

"I'll be there in a minute," Heather said, hanging up.

She saw the crew working on the lawn. One of them edged the sidewalk as another used a leaf blower to sweep up the grass clippings. Bobby rode by on a riding lawnmower. It appeared to be efficient business as usual.

Heather pulled into the drive and waved to get Bobby's attention. She saw the curtain move in her mother's living room window. Bonnie wasn't covert in her spying.

Bobby rode the mower toward her before shutting off the engine. He was a barrel-chested man with a thick gray beard that hung down over his old t-shirt. "Howdy, Mrs. Harrison."

"Hey, Bobby." Heather smiled as she made a show of checking the lawn. "Looks good."

"Yes, ma'am," Bobby agreed.

Heather again watched the curtain move. She turned her body so her mother wouldn't be able to see her face. There was no reason to risk Bonnie lip reading what she said.

"Has my mom given you any trouble?" Heather asked. "I mean since we talked last time?"

"Nothing I'd complain about," Bobby said. He turned to look at the house and chuckled. The curtain shifted. "She keeps a close eye on us. I make sure not to look in her direction when I'm on the mower."

"I'm still sorry about that. Thank you for being understanding of her eccentricities," Heather said.

Her mother had demanded she fire them for peeping after she'd caught Bobby glancing at the house while he was on the riding mower. In her mind, the mower had put him high enough to see into her living room. At least Bonnie hadn't accused him of being in prison to his face. Yet.

"It's no problem. She's your mother, Mrs. Harrison. No need to apologize for her."

Heather sighed. If only that were true.

"Listen." Heather put her hands on her hips. "I hate that I have to mention this, but she overheard one of you joking about dropping soap in the shower.

Now, I'm going to give you a stern look and appear mad."

"I understand." Bobby hooked his thumbs into his front pockets and hung his head down.

"Can you please ask the guys not to make prison jokes where she might be able to overhear? Or any jokes for that matter?" Heather asked.

"Can do." Bobby nodded.

"Thanks." Heather lifted her finger and shook it at him.

"Would it help if I started crying a little?" He asked, hiding his smirk. "You can hit me a couple of times if you want."

"Let's not oversell it." Heather had to suppress her laughter. "Oh, hey, while we're here, is there any chance you can add Anderson House to your route for me? Do the basics and write me an estimate and plan for saving that backyard?"

"I drove by it yesterday hoping you'd ask," Bobby admitted. "I already have some ideas. I can get out there Wednesday to measure."

"Perfect." Heather dropped her arms to the side and said, "You're a good man, Bobby. Thank you."

"Yes, ma'am." Bobby winked at her before kicking his foot on the ground like a scolded child.

"Now I have to go tell my mom you're not an

escaped convict." Heather sighed. Yep, this was her life.

"For the record, it wasn't prison. It was jail. DUI. Me and some of the boys got drunk and decided instead of driving we'd borrow a few horses and ride them home like cowboys."

"Cowboys?" Heather arched an eyebrow. Bobby didn't exactly look like the up-on-a-horse type. "You got charged for driving a horse while intoxicated?"

He patted his stomach. "Yeah, who'd have thought. The horses did most of the steering. That was about sixty pounds and sixteen years ago."

"I see."

"We didn't hurt anything, and I think they would have let us off with a warning, but Grandpa wasn't exactly the forgiving type. It was a small town, and he had his buddy the sheriff throw us in jail for the night to teach us a lesson."

Bobby shuffled his feet as he went back to the mower.

Heather wasn't surprised when the front door to her mother's home opened before she could touch the doorknob. Bonnie Warrick waved her daughter inside. The ceiling lights were dimmed, and with the curtains closed it became difficult to see.

"Mom, what are you doing in the dark?" Heather crossed over to a lamp and turned it on.

"You told me to close the curtains when they come by," her mother stated.

"Wow, okay," Heather muttered.

"I wasn't expecting you to come by today," Bonnie said. "This is a nice surprise."

Heather refused to point out that her mother had called her minutes before to complain. "Well, I wanted to see you. I've missed you. How've you been?"

Bonnie made a small noise and waved her hand. "You know me. I'm never one to complain."

"Speaking of which, I spoke to the guys. They won't be making any more inappropriate jokes when they're over here. Of course, I checked them thoroughly before hiring them." Heather patted her mother's arm. "They might not be funny, but the lawn does look nice, don't you think? I ran into Mrs. Jennings at the market the other day, and she asked if I'd give her Bobby's number. I think she's jealous of how your hedges are trimmed."

That perked her mother's mood. Mrs. Jennings and her mother had been locked in a strange nicety war ever since Heather could remember. They smiled and flattered each other, but the words never really sounded like a compliment. Each Christmas they would try to outdo each other's lawn decorations, and each summer they tried to compete for the best flower garden award.

"You didn't give it to her, I hope," Bonnie crossed to the curtains and pulled them to the side, not hiding the fact she looked at the lawn. "It does look good, doesn't it?"

"I wouldn't dare give her the number. I told her they were booked solid," Heather answered.

"Good girl." Bonnie nodded in approval. "That woman is always trying to steal my ideas. Whoever said imitation is the biggest form of flattery was a complete idiot."

"It was good seeing you. I'm sorry I can't stay longer, but I have a lot of work—"

"Oh, wait, I have something for you." Bonnie crossed to a sideboard and pulled out an envelope. "I found these, and I thought you might want to go through them."

Heather lifted the flap to the envelope to see the top edge of a stack of photos. She began to reach inside to pull them out.

"They're of our boy," her mother stated. Lightly reaching to touch the envelope before retracting her fingers. "He would have grown up to be such a handsome young man."

Heather pushed the photos back down, only catching a glimpse of the top of a head. Her heart squeezed in her chest. She had not been expecting this.

"Do you ever talk to Ben?" Bonnie asked. "Maybe we should send him some copies. What do you think?"

"Uh, yeah, maybe." Heather closed the envelope flap. She held them tight. "I'll take care of it."

"Don't you want to look—"

"Mom, I would, but I have so much work I need to do. I just wanted to drop by and say hello." The envelope felt like fire in her hand. Her ring vibrated, and she felt her magic trying to build as her emotions fought for an outlet. The last thing she wanted to do was spend the afternoon crying on her mother's couch and talking about what might have been. Bonnie would try to comfort her, but would inevitably criticize the Warrick beliefs, or start in on how Heather was still young enough—barely—to give her more grandchildren. "Maybe we can get together for lunch this weekend? What do you think?"

Together-time in a public space would be a better bet for both of them.

"This weekend?" She was shaking her head before the words even finished leaving her mouth. "I can't this weekend. I promised Mary I'd go shopping with her Saturday."

"Ah, that's too bad. Maybe another time." Heather hurried to the door before it could occur to her mother to ask her to go shopping with them. She opened the door, calling as she stepped out of the house, "Love you. Call you later."

CHAPTER SIX

"This place is amazing." Lorna walked through the ground floor level of Anderson House on a self-guided tour. She went up the stairs to the first landing and disappeared. Heather heard her going back down the second set of steps toward the kitchen.

"Did you bring everything?" Heather asked Vivien, glancing at one of the bags she carried.

"Book, candles, wine," Vivien answered. She patted the messenger bag. "I had vodka, but Lorna took it out."

Heather chuckled. "Can't say I blame her."

"Yeah, me either." Vivien gestured to the second bag. "She made cupcakes, so we'll have sugar after."

Sugar always helped replenish their energy after

a séance. Calling forth spirits could be physically and emotionally draining. Besides, any excuse to eat cupcakes was a good excuse.

Vivien glanced around and set the bags on the floor. "It looks bigger empty. What did you do with all the old furniture that was left in here?"

"A couple of the pieces I found shoved in a storage closet are being restored. The rest are in my storage unit." Heather frowned as she thought about it and pulled the notepad out of her back pocket to jot down a note to plan a storage unit sale. Every time she bought a new property, all of the treasures left over from former residents were transferred to storage to go through later. Only, later never really came. "Actually, it's in my second storage unit. I'm beginning to look like a hoarder."

"I hear your cry for help," Vivien stated. "I know an auctioneer. We'll set up a meeting. You tell his team what's going, and they'll organize the whole thing and hand you a check at the end of it."

"How do you know an auctioneer?" Heather arched a brow. "You've never mentioned that before."

"You don't know everything about me," Vivien answered. "I have secrets. I'm a lady of great mystery."

"This coming from the woman who's told me about every single one night stand she's ever had in her life whether I wanted to hear about it or not." Heather chuckled. Before she had met Troy, Vivien hadn't been shy about enjoying a varied sex life.

"You love my stories." Vivien grinned. Ever since she'd allowed herself to admit her feelings for Troy, there had been a shift inside Vivien. She'd always been vivacious and fun, but also a little erratic and wild. Now, whenever Heather touched her, there was a calm undercurrent to Vivien's emotions. Troy's easygoing nature acted like a stabilizing force to Vivien's whirlwind.

"I do love your stories," Heather admitted. A tiny pang of lonely jealousy hit her, and she instantly suppressed it. She was happy for her friends, and her brother.

"And I love this house." Lorna came from the opposite direction, having moved around the downstairs in a circular pattern. "Boss, can I get an advance on my paycheck? I want to take out a mortgage."

"I'll look into it." Heather laughed. "Want to see the rest?"

"Yes, please." Lorna instantly went to the stairs, reached the halfway mark, and turned the corner to go up the rest of the way instead of back down into the kitchen like before. The evening sky darkened the stained-glass window. A light came on upstairs as Lorna reached the top.

Vivien lifted the bag and asked, "Where are we setting this up?"

"Second floor." Heather ran her hand over the railing as she climbed to follow Lorna. "That's where I felt the activity."

"Still want the house, Lorna?" Vivien called. "It could be haunted."

"That's why you should move in with me," Lorna teased. "We can all live here. One floor for each of us."

"Dibs on the kitchen," Vivien said.

"I imagine you'd want to move in with my brother at some point." Heather stood near the top of the stairs as Lorna explored the home.

"He can live on my floor," Lorna answered, disappearing to explore one of the bedrooms.

"I don't really want to live with my brother again," Heather said, remembering what it had been like when they were kids. She'd seen ghosts, and he'd been more like their mother—anti-supernatural everything. Though, to be fair to William, he had changed a lot in adulthood.

"What?" Vivien put the bag on the floor next to Heather before lifting her hands to encompass the room. "You don't think William's pleather couches and football posters would look great in here?"

"Where is my brother tonight anyway?" Heather asked. He rarely left Lorna's side if he could help it.

"I told him we are having a girls' night," Lorna answered. "I promised to call if we did anything dangerous. I think he only half believed me."

"Just picture it," Vivien continued as if they hadn't digressed from her teasing. "Flat-screen television in every room. Teal pleather as far as the eye can see. Mini fridges installed on each floor with a microwave on top. Maybe a beer keg fridge. Posters of chicks in bikinis held up by pushpins—"

"Hey, no, he doesn't have half-naked women on his walls," Lorna protested as she crossed to the bedroom Jan had been playing tic-tac-toe in earlier.

"You didn't know teenage William," Heather said. "What was the name of that woman on the car in the music video? The one he—"

"Heather, Viv," Lorna called, sounding concerned.

They instantly rushed to the room to join her.

Lorna stood next to where the tic-tac-toe boards had been drawn on the floor. Someone had swiped them away. She held a piece of paper that looked as if it had been crumpled then smoothed. "Look what I found."

Lorna turned the page to show a child's drawing on it. Heather stiffened. It looked like a picture of her if the hair and style of clothing was any indication. It was the same pattern and color of the shirt she'd had on earlier in the day. In the picture, Heather stood in front of Anderson House crying while it was on fire. Blue tears dropped and gathered in a puddle at her feet.

"What the hell?" Vivien demanded, snatching the page from Lorna. "Who drew this? Where did you find it?"

"Shoved behind that plaster bucket," Lorna said. "I don't know why I checked there. I just did."

"Because that's your power. You're a finder," Heather said.

"But I wasn't consciously looking for a picture," Lorna said. "Every other time I had to be thinking about what I wanted to find. It took concentration. I found this just walking into the room."

"Your gifts are becoming stronger, like ours," Heather said.

"Heather, do you know where this might have come from?" Vivien asked.

She frowned. "I have an idea."

Jan. Who else could it be? The girl was the only child that had been in the house—or at least Heather could reasonably assume so—since Heather had bought the property.

"Well?" Lorna prompted. "Who drew it?"

"Martin Edwards' daughter, January." Heather took the picture from Vivien and carefully folded it before shoving it in her back pocket. She had no idea what she was going to do with it. As a parent, she would have wanted to be told if her son had been drawing disturbing things. As the subject of the drawing, she wasn't sure how to broach the subject with Martin. Things were already awkward between them.

"Martin, the cute contractor?" Vivien asked.

"Wait, isn't that the kid you said you saw in the truck and you thought... uh, saw in the truck?" Lorna asked.

"Yes. The one whose reflection on the glass I thought was my son's," Heather answered, saying the words Lorna refused to finish. She thought about what Julia had started to tell her.

"What?" Vivien demanded.

"Julia indicated that it might not be my son, but a warning from my magic to get my attention."

Heather thought of Jan. She seemed like a sweet kid —precocious and strong willed sure, but sweet.

"Do you think something is wrong with the girl?" Vivien asked.

"Of course not, she's just a child," Heather denied. Anything else was unthinkable.

"I'm not a child phycologist, but as far as I'm concerned, she's thinking of setting this house on fire," Vivien insisted. "That says disturbed to me. What do you know about her?"

"Not a lot. Jan's sweet," Heather said. Was Vivien right? Was there something wrong with the girl? "Her mom died when she was born. She's articulate and smart, a little sassy. I can tell her father loves her. He said she's a tomboy and likes working on the houses with him."

"What else?" Lorna's voice was softer than Vivien's, but she could hear the concern in the tone.

"Martin told me that he has her in an online school, not public. He said she was imaginative and did better that way, and that her teachers didn't appreciate how she was. I assumed it meant that she learned differently and thrived better at home." Heather tried to dismiss the sense of worry building inside her.

"Or that he knows something is wrong with her, and he's trying to control it," Vivien said.

"Let's not gossip about a ten-year-old girl." Heather furrowed her brow. "This isn't us."

"Fighting demons wasn't us either until we summoned one and it attacked Lorna," Vivien countered.

"Do you honestly think that Martin's daughter is a demon?" Heather shook her head, not buying it. "She's just a kid."

"Who knows what kind of things can get in during tragic events?" Vivien countered.

"What does that even mean?" Heather frowned.

Vivien began to pace as she tried to reason. "Maybe all the emotion and panic surrounding her mother's death let something undesirable slip inside the baby. Julia was able to slip inside of me and wear me like a skin suit. I had no control over my body. Maybe it's like that. Maybe she can't control it."

"We're talking about a real girl here," Heather insisted. "Not some horror movie plot. Julia was able to slip inside of you because we're..." She held up her forefinger to show the ring. "Because we're us. And you're implying something lived inside Jan for over a decade. Julia is the most powerful ghost I know, and she could only keep you for a few minutes."

"If you won't take an otherworldly answer, then maybe it's simpler than that." Vivien crossed her arms over her chest. "All psychopaths were children once. I'm sure their parents thought they were great too. You see it on the news all the time. Some bewildered neighbor going on about how they didn't understand how this could happen because he was such a nice, respectable man. Well, that nice, respectable serial killer was a kid once probably setting fires, and doing God knows what else."

"Now you're saying Jan is a budding serial killer?" Heather mimicked Vivien's defensive posture.

"Or a firebug," Vivien said. "She's clearly fantasizing about pyromania. This is a reason to be concerned."

"Oh, hey, come on ladies," Lorna interrupted. "There is no reason for this to get heated. I raised three kids. My boys were always doing stupid things in order to shock people. Even my daughter sometimes did. This could just be some expression of anger. Maybe she resents that her dad has to work and wishes the house would burn down so he'd have more time with her. Ten-year-olds aren't always the most logical creatures. Or, if what Vivien's psychic senses have been picking up is true, then maybe Jan realizes that she might be competing for her father's attention and—"

"She would have no reason to think that Martin and I are anything more than employer and contractor," Heather denied. "I'm not dating him."

"Yet," Vivien said.

"Ever," Heather insisted.

"Why? Because you're his boss?" Vivien laughed. "So what? Like that scenario has never been played out. Because he's a dad? You're great with kids."

"Either she's a demon-possessed serial killer or a great kid," Heather said. "You can't have it both ways."

"I said *you're* great *with* kids. I didn't say she was a great kid." Vivien walked toward the door. "I don't know her. I'm reserving my opinion but erring on the side of caution because I love you, and I'm worried."

"There is another possibility," Lorna said, following Vivien out of the room. "The same reason we're here, to detect if something is haunting the house that Heather can't see. Maybe that is who drew the picture. You said someone was drawing in the dust."

"If a ghost had enough energy and time, it's possible they could learn to manipulate all the elements it takes to draw." Heather spoke loudly so they could hear her. "From what I've seen, though, affecting the physical world isn't easy for spirits."

Exhaustion tried to settle over her shoulders. Heather hated the not knowing. Part of her wished she could run away, and the other part wanted to bury her head in work and not think. She wanted to go from task to task to task, checking them off her notebook checklist.

"I don't feel like there is a presence," Vivien said. "Not that it means anything. Heather, do you sense anyone with us?"

"No." Heather gave one last look around the room. The temperature was normal, and nothing formed in the dust. She joined Lorna and Vivien on the landing. "All I felt earlier was a chill. That's why I asked you both to help me try to locate it. If a ghost has been stirred from the construction, I want to know what we're dealing with here. Maybe we can send it on its way."

Vivien had the messenger bag open. Julia's séance book had been wrapped in blue cloth and was sitting in the middle of the floor. Vivien began peeling back the edges of the material.

The handmade, three inches thick tome had been part of Heather's inheritance, one she only learned about recently. Julia had hidden it underneath the stage at the theater. The padded leather cover was embossed with a circular pattern of symbols. Three of the symbols matched their three rings. She wasn't sure what they meant. If she had to guess, Vivien's would stand for her intuitiveness, Lorna's would have something to do with the fact she was a healer and a finder, and Heather's would have to be the magic she inherited from her grandmother.

Vivien smoothed the cloth underneath the book. Lorna had drawn the same pattern on the fabric that was on the book cover. As the material lay on the floor, it gave a larger séancing area. The first time they'd tried, the ghost had been trapped in the circle on top of the book and couldn't move around. Julia had suggested a larger space might make spirits more agreeable since no one enjoyed being pinned down.

Vivien set four blue candles around the edge of the material before anointing them with basil oil from a small vial. Heather wasn't sure why it worked, but the blue color helped them amplify their messages to the dead when doing a séance, and the basil oil provided protection. And, honestly, after they'd accidentally summoned a demon, they could use all the protection they could get. The energy from bad-tempered spirits could open the veil just enough to let demonic figures through with them.

Lorna went to the food bag and pulled out two plastic containers. She lifted the first and said, "Cupcakes for after."

"Yum," Heather answered.

Lorna put the cupcakes back inside, then lifted the second container, and said, "Blueberry scones for now. Since blueberries are supposed to help against psychic attacks, I thought it couldn't hurt."

"Gimme," Vivien said, reaching up from her place on the floor.

Lorna opened the container and took out a napkin wrapped scone.

"Heather, I think you should consider living with us. Lorna is the best roommate in the world." Vivien unwrapped her scone and took a bite. With a full mouth, she said, "She comes with so many snacks. If she moves in here, I'm so coming too."

"What about Troy?" Heather asked. She sat across from Vivien. The hard floor wasn't the most comfortable position, but she had other things on her mind.

"He'd be invited to visit." Vivien chuckled. "Hos before bros."

"Um, I don't think that works for us." Lorna handed a scone to Heather before taking one for herself and returning the container to the bag.

"Chicks before dicks," Vivien amended, toasting her scone in the air.

"Yes, much classier," Lorna drawled sarcastically. She remained standing. "Thank you."

"Ass before class," Vivien said.

"Time to take your rhyming dictionary away," Lorna stated.

"Carbs before anything else," Heather said, biting into the scone. She instantly moaned. "Omigod, Lorna, you need to open a restaurant. In my kitchen."

"Yes!" Vivien exclaimed. "I'll buy a space for you, and you can run it however you want. But I want a reserved corner booth."

Vivien owned several fast food businesses in North Carolina. With her psychic abilities, she had a natural talent for picking winning locations and loyal staff members.

Lorna shook her head. "I don't think it would be fun to cook for strangers on that scale. I like cooking for friends and family. Someone once told me that the surest way to kill your love of something is to turn it into a job."

"I don't think that's true. I love restoring homes like this one." Heather thought about it for a moment. "I maybe don't love being a landlord sometimes."

"More pizza box hoarders?" Lorna asked.

"Oh, don't remind me. That poor man. I don't think I told you both what happened. The cleaner I hired to help him had a family emergency out of town. She forgot to tell me she was quitting." Heather sighed. Mr. Willis was an elderly tenant who lived on a fixed income. When left alone, he didn't take the best care of himself. "And, of course, he didn't want to complain."

"I was only joking," Lorna said, sounding concerned. "Did he fall into old habits?"

Heather nodded. "Yep. Twenty-eight empty pizza boxes stacked in the basement and counting. It's all the man will eat when no one is there to cook for him. I've got a help wanted ad for someone to take over cleaning and cooking."

Heather didn't make money off that particular property. After taxes and paying for the cleaning service, the place barely broke even. She would never tell Mr. Willis that. Why should she? He'd worked hard his entire life and had great pride in taking care of himself. She hoped that if she needed help when she was older, someone would be able to give it.

"Want me to help interview?" Vivien asked.

"Yes, please. Your insight would be a great help." Heather nodded, taking another bite. "Mm, these are amazing, Lorna."

"Thank you." Lorna opened the container and lifted it. "Want another?"

"Yes." Vivien snagged one even though she was offering them to Heather.

Heather grabbed a second.

"Give me his address. I'll run meals by there before work each day until you can find someone," Lorna offered.

"That would be amazing," Heather said.

"Oh, I brought pillows for us to sit on just in case. I'll be right back." Lorna went down the stairs.

Vivien finished her second scone and leaned forward to open the front cover of Julia's book. The insides were handwritten in beautiful calligraphy, from the title page that read *"Warrick"* to the lists of names and dates logging the séances Heather's grandmother had performed.

Vivien stopped at the séance listings. "These are always so sad." She ran her finger over the decorative border lining the page and read aloud, "December 9, 1928, Fiona O'Leary, six dollars to contact three-year-old daughter Mirabella. Not earthbound."

"I know. So many deaths," Heather agreed.

"When I touch the book, it's almost like I can sense all of them," Vivien said. "It's getting stronger. I thought my psychic tendencies would have leveled off by now, but ever since I found this ring, they just keep growing."

Vivien tried to keep her tone light, but Heather could detect her concern. The first time they'd looked inside, Vivien had called it a book of death filled with the pain of tremendous loss.

"It's the same for me. Ghosts are getting louder too." Heather touched the ring on her forefinger. "When I took the ring off, it did become harder for me to hear Julia. If it's too much, maybe we take the rings off and put them away."

"We can't, not yet," Lorna appeared, holding three pillows. She shared a look with Vivien. "Not until we help you, Heather, like you helped us."

Heather knew her friends thought there was something they could do for her, but there wasn't. Not when it came to her pain. She had tried to explain it, but the depth of her convictions never seemed to make it all the way through to them. They understood, felt where she was coming from, but they held out hope that the path would reveal itself.

"I think I forgot the lighter," Vivien said. She flipped through the pages of the book until she reached the list of incantations. She pointed at one and said, "In case anyone needs the refresher."

"I'm pretty sure we won't need it." Lorna dropped a pillow on the floor near her feet and then handed the other two over to her friends.

Heather slipped the cushion under her butt and nodded in appreciation. "Thanks."

"You take such good care of us," Vivien added, with a grin.

"I do my best." Lorna moved the food bag out of the way and set it beside the wall in between two of the bedroom doors.

"You *are* the best," Heather corrected. She turned her attention to the book and inhaled a deep, slow breath. "Okay, let's get to it. Here goes nothing. I'm ready if you are."

CHAPTER SEVEN

"Our intent is to talk to any spirits inhabiting this home," Heather stated, stretching her hands toward Lorna and Vivien. They formed a circle around the book. She kept her eyes on the candles, wondering if they would light themselves. As if answering her silent question, the wicks caught in a small burst of flames the second they joined hands.

"That will never get old," Vivien whispered.

Energy flowed through Heather from their clasped hands as their magic built. Lorna's and Vivien's emotions mingled with her own as they joined in spirit. The tingling caused her hair to lift from her shoulders, sending a shiver of goosebumps over her entire body.

Vivien always had a sense of excitement and

enthusiasm in whatever she did. That did not change with séancing. If anything, Vivien seemed worried about Lorna. After being married for twenty years and a mother of three kids, Lorna had developed the tendency to put everyone else's feelings and needs before her own. Out of the three of them, she'd be the one to say yes to something even though she wasn't convinced it was a good idea.

The last time they'd tried this Lorna had been more hesitant, but since seeing Vivien make peace with her dead husband, Lorna had become much more comfortable in what they were doing. However, the underlying fear was still there.

Heather knew what they would feel from her. It was the same every time. They focused on the hard knot in her chest that formed a thick shell around her pain. Since that is what was always the most prevalent inside her, that is what they sensed. It eased a little when they shared the burden of it with her, but she didn't want to let go. That pain represented her love for her son. There was nothing that could compare to such a loss.

The overhead lights flickered as expected. Ghosts needed to borrow the energy to manifest, and they would take it however they could—whether it was a group of highly emotional people during a séance or the city's power grid.

"Ready?" Vivien whispered.

Lorna and Heather nodded.

Together they said, "We open the door between two worlds to call forth any spirits inhabiting this home. Come back from the grave so that we may hear. Come back from the grave and show yourself to us so that all may see. Come back from the grave and answer for what you have done so that you may be judged."

Tiny lights formed over the book like fireflies, swarming around. The ring on her finger sent a pulse of energy through her, which then traveled to her friends through their connected hands. The lights multiplied in number, appearing trapped within transparent feet. The shoes looked to belong to a man, as did the trousers.

The lights suddenly veered off course and shot to the side where they multiplied and clustered. A second figure began to form. The lights shot to the side again, illuminating a third person. They were all contained in the cloth circle.

"What's happening?" Lorna asked.

Heather shook her head to indicate she didn't know, unable to answer as she watched.

"I think we got three..." Vivien gasped as the light broke off again. "No four spirits."

The lights broke off yet another time.

"Five," Lorna whispered. "There's not enough room for them all."

"Six," Vivien said. "This is getting crowded."

Lorna jerked her hands from the circle as a spirit appeared close to where she was sitting. They'd learned that once they started, their hands did not need to be joined for the séance to continue. Simply letting go would not send the spirits away.

The light from the candles replicated, becoming trapped beneath the ghosts' surfaces. It reflected up their bodies, revealing four men and two women.

"Oh, crap," Vivien whispered, crawling around the circle to be closer to Heather. Lorna appeared next to her other side. "That's a lot of ghosts—"

The lights separated again and began bouncing off the invisible boundary of the circle. The spirits started to move, fighting their crowded space. Hundreds of tiny lights became thousands, shining over the dim room. The lights stopped flickering as the ghosts took over.

Suddenly, a single speck of light shot out of the circle. It instantly multiplied to reveal a spirit outside of the containment area before breaking off to do it again. As the ghosts brightened, they turned their attention toward the three women.

"Shit," Vivien whispered. "They've escaped."

"What do we do?" Lorna asked.

"Ten, eleven, twelve—there are so many of them," Vivien said. "Thirteen."

"Where did they come from?" Lorna asked.

"So many... Why didn't I feel them?" Heather added, half in awe and half in fear. She always assumed her strong gifts meant she knew when a spirit was nearby. Never had she imagined so many ghosts could be around her when she didn't feel them.

Vivien stood, pulling Heather to her feet. Heather, in turn, pulled Lorna. They backed toward the bathroom.

"Spirits you have been found pure. We release you into the light. Go in peace and love," Heather commanded.

In response, a few of the lights danced upward like the dying embers of a bonfire. However, even more remained. Some of the spirits looked angry. Others looked confused. The annoying woman who'd asked for her help pointed at Heather and laughed.

"Spirits you have been found pure," Vivien

stated loudly. "We release you into the light. Go in peace and love."

Another one left like dying embers.

"Lorna, you try," Heather said, hoping they'd listen to her.

"Spirits you have been found pure. We release you into the light. Go in peace and love," Lorna ordered.

Two more left, but that meant a half dozen spirits remained.

"Shit," Vivien stated, grabbing Heather's arm and squeezing tight. "Shit."

"Not helping," Heather countered.

Lorna grabbed Heather's hand and held it.

"Shit," Vivien swore.

"What do we—" Lorna began.

"Jan!" Martin's shout came from downstairs. "January, are you in here?"

As if breaking the spell, the ghosts scattered and disappeared. The overhead lights came back on, and the candles blew out. The three women stood clustered together.

"What was that?" Vivien demanded.

"Who is that yelling?" Lorna asked at the same time.

The sound of heavy footsteps came up the stairs.

Martin appeared in sweatpants, a worn t-shirt, and sneakers. His dark hair was wet and slicked back on his head away from his face.

"Jan, are...?" Martin's eyes stopped on the cloth and books before lifting to meet Heather's. "Oh, I, uh..." He slowed his steps as he again looked down at the fabric. "I'm sorry. I'm looking for my daughter. She ran off, and I had a feeling she might be... Her bike is by the back door, and the house was open. She likes the tower. Have you seen her—*what is this?*"

His confusion got the better of him as he pointed at the floor.

"Dad!" Jan cried, running down from the third floor. Her little feet sounded on the steps. She rushed at him, throwing her arms around him as if terrified.

"Where did she come from?" Lorna whispered. "How much did she hear?"

Heather stiffened. Was Jan in the house the whole time? She must have been. They would have seen her pass by to the third floor. Had she heard what they had been saying about her?

"How much did she see?" Vivien added, just as softly.

"Shit." Now it was Heather's turn to cuss. "I don't know."

"What is going on here?" Martin held his daughter close. "What is all this stuff?"

"Girls night slumber party," Vivien explained, hardly convincing.

"Hi, Martin, we haven't met." Lorna held out her hand. "I'm a friend of Heather's, Lorna Addams." She smiled at Jan, who didn't turn to look. "And you must be January. Such a pretty name."

Martin didn't take her offered hand but instead nodded as he kept his hands on his daughter's back. Lorna dropped the offer with a tiny lift of her fingers to acknowledge his nod.

"This is Vivien," Lorna introduced, trying to sound friendly.

"We've met," Martin said.

"We're..." Heather tried to think of a convincing lie.

"They took them." Jan's shoulders shook as if she were about to cry.

"We took what?" Vivien asked.

"I'm sorry. She shouldn't have broken in," Martin said, ushering his daughter toward the stairs. When she didn't cooperate, he lifted her in his arms and carried her. "She knows better. I'll have a talk with her. It won't happen again."

"It's all right," Heather said, following him. Well,

actually, it wasn't all right for Jan to be roaming a remodel by herself at night or running away from home. Martin had his hands full.

When they reached the first floor, he set Jan down and walked her toward the door.

"They took my friends," Jan told her dad. Tears had rolled down her cheeks when she looked at Heather in anger.

"Martin, wait," Heather insisted. If the girl overheard them, she needed to know how much. "What's she talking about?"

"Nothing," Martin dismissed. "She's just imaginative."

"No, Dad, I'm not. I know—"

"Quiet," Martin ordered softly. He looked tired, almost defeated as if he'd been fighting a neverending battle for a long time. "Don't do this here, Jan. We'll talk about it at home."

"Please, just..." Heather looked between father and daughter. It wasn't her place to butt in, but she couldn't stop herself. She saw Martin's frustration and the girl's pain.

Heather went to Jan and knelt on the floor in front of her. The girl took a step back.

"Jan, your friends, what do they look like?" Heather asked.

"I'm not supposed to encourage—" Martin began.

"Let her answer," Vivien interrupted from the landing near the stained-glass window as she gazed down at them. She nodded at Heather, giving her a meaningful look. "We can help."

"Jan?" Heather prompted. "Can you describe them to me?"

"They're not real," Martin stated. "My daughter has a vivid imagination. It's normal for kids to have imaginary friends."

"Do you think that they are imaginary, sweetheart?" Heather asked, keeping her attention focused on the child.

Jan looked at her father, as if not wanting to go against what he was saying.

"I promise, you can tell me," Heather said. "My mom used to tell me I had imaginary friends, too."

"We're leaving," Martin pushed lightly at Jan's shoulder to turn her toward the door.

"Like people," Jan said.

Martin stopped pushing.

"They look like people you can see through, and they talk funny," Jan said.

Heather glanced to where Lorna had joined

Vivien on the small landing. She closed her eyes and took a deep breath.

Oh, fuck.

When she opened her eyes, she saw herself reflected in Jan's expression. She remembered that fear, that feeling of loneliness because no one understood. At that age, she'd had her grandmother to explain things to her. Jan had no one.

"See, imaginary friends. She's creative," Martin rationalized. "I should get her home."

Heather reached up to touch Martin's arm. Her eye met his dark ones. "Please, I think we can help."

His mouth opened as if he would protest, but through the contact of their touch, she detected a sad desperation in him. He'd probably been fighting and struggling with this for a long time.

"Are you talking about ghosts?" Heather asked Jan.

The girl looked at her father before slowly nodding. "They're my friends."

"We see them too," Vivien stated.

Heather would not have said it as bluntly as her friend. She looked up at Martin for a reaction. He appeared as if he didn't know what to say. Heather couldn't blame him. Not many people understood the supernatural.

Heather let her hand fall away from him as she reached toward Jan. "Viv's right, you know, we've seen them."

She kept her eyes on the child, not wanting to see what had to be Martin's obvious disbelief. If he didn't believe his daughter, how could she expect he'd believe her?

"I see them," Heather said.

"You do?" Jan's expression lost some of its anger.

Heather nodded. "Since I was little, like you."

"This isn't..." Martin began. "I mean, we can't..."

"It's going to be all right," Vivien assured him.

"This isn't a joke," Martin stated.

"Trust me, that I know." Heather inched forward and then reached to push back a strand of Jan's hair from her face. "People don't listen when you try to tell them, do they?"

Jan shook her head in denial. "They say I'm making it up."

"I know you're not making it up, sweetie." Heather put her hand on the girl's shoulder. Usually when it came to others, only Vivien sensed what they felt. Heather had never been clairsentient or claircognizant. Yet somehow with Martin and his daughter, she felt a trickle of what they were going through. Martin was worried, as any

118

parent would be. Jan had a wall built around her and lived in her own world—presumably with her ghost friends.

That last fact worried her. Ghosts needed energy to manifest. Heather knew from firsthand experience how much they could take from a person sensitive to their presence, how much they could demand. She had to learn to control it, but she had help. Julia had been there to teach her. Jan had no one.

"Most adults didn't listen to me either," Heather said. "They thought I made up stories."

"You really see them?" Jan turned her attention to Vivien and Lorna. A sense of hope and relief came over the girl at the idea.

"Not like Heather, but we can with help," Lorna answered.

Heather let her hand fall away from Jan, feeling like she was eavesdropping on her emotions. "I had a grandma who understood the truth because she saw them too. You see, you're not alone. I'm going to tell you what she told me. She said, most people fear what they don't understand, and they have a difficult time believing because they can't see. That doesn't make them bad, so you can't be mad at them for it. We're special. We've been blessed with a gift. That means we have to be extra careful because we have a responsibility to the dead. They're trusting us to keep their secrets."

Jan nodded.

"One of those secrets is that they're here," Heather said. She had always resented the advice, but it had made her life easier as a girl. "You have to stop telling those who can't see that they're with us."

Jan frowned. "But that's lying. I do see them."

It was like talking to her past self. Heather took a deep breath. "I know. I know it doesn't make sense now, but I need you to trust me. Keeping this secret will help."

Jan gave a halfhearted nod.

"Do they sometimes get loud?" Heather asked. "Like a dozen people screaming at once?"

Jan nodded. "They want me to do things for them. They make it hard to sleep."

"I can help you learn to quiet them," Heather said.

"I've heard enough." Martin leaned over to take his daughter's hand. "I'm sure you mean well, but this isn't... This... I'm going to have to trust the doctors on this one." He gave a slight tug. "Come on, Jan. It's time for bed."

"But I want to—"

"Bed." Martin pushed open the front door and

walked her out. Heather didn't see his truck, so she assumed he'd parked around back where he'd seen her bike.

"Negotiate," Jan countered.

"No. Get in the truck. And don't think we're not going to talk about you running off." He strode around the side of the house. Jan glanced back at Heather before running after him.

Vivien and Lorna appeared next to her.

"I take it back," Vivien said. "She's not a monster."

"I hope she didn't hear us talking about the picture," Lorna added.

"She didn't," Vivien assured them. "She mostly seemed frightened, then relieved. I don't think she's ever met anyone who believed her before."

"That has to be awful," Lorna said. She stepped back into the house. Vivien and Heather followed her. "Though, I can't blame Martin. Until I moved to Freewild Cove, if one of my kids had told me they were seeing people who weren't there and hearing voices, I would have taken them to see the doctor, too. I wouldn't have believed them."

"I don't think he believed us, either," Heather said. "Did you see his face?"

"He wanted to." Vivien bit her lip and turned to the stairs. "I'll pick up."

"What is it?" Heather grabbed her arm to stop her. "What aren't you telling me?"

"You don't want to hear it." Vivien's concern flowed through their connection.

"Try me. Is it something about Jan?" Heather insisted.

Vivien stepped away so that Heather had to let go. "All I say is that you should pay more attention to Martin."

"Is he dangerous?" Heather returned to the door to look out.

"Only to your maidenhead," Vivien muttered.

"What?" Heather spun back around.

"Nothing." Vivien's voice was forcefully cheerful. "Going to pick up our mess now."

"Don't you dare take another step," Heather demanded, following her toward the stairs. If there was something off about Martin, she wanted to know. "Explain."

Lorna chuckled and moved to go past Vivien. "How about I clean up?"

"I'm just saying it's been so long that the cobwebs probably sewed your hymen back together," Vivien stated. "I think they call it virginating."

"*Revirgination*," Lorna corrected. "Hymenorrha-phy. It's a real thing."

"I'm terrified that you know that," Vivien said.

"Daytime talk shows." Lorna stopped on her way upstairs to remain in the conversation.

"Why the hell would anyone want to be a virgin again?" Vivien asked with a small shiver. "All that fumbling and, *ugh*, no one knew what they were doing back then. It was awkward and weird and uncomfortable."

"I know, right? They did a whole show on the subject. Born again virgins." Lorna frowned. "It all seems very medieval to me. Why would a woman want a man specifically looking to marry a virgin? I mean, out of the three of us, I'm prob-ably the biggest prude and I don't get it. That should be low on the list of considerations. If a woman is, great for her, her choice. If she's not, starting a relationship by lying about it isn't a good start."

"If the man is obsessed with virginity over every other quality, then I think the police need to take a deeper look into his psyche..." Vivien held up her hands. "Or his basement. Just saying."

"Hey, queens of digression, why in the world are you talking about this? The whole turn of conversation is disturbing," Heather said. "And nice try you two at trying to avoid answering me."

"Who's avoiding? I tell you to get laid all the time," Vivien quipped. "I even offered to hire a gigolo for you."

"That wasn't a gigolo. That was a man in a speedo on the beach," Heather corrected.

"Practically the same thing," Vivien dismissed.

"I don't know why I have to keep telling you that I'm perfectly happy being single. I have a full life." Heather moved past Lorna and Vivien to go upstairs to clean. "We should be thinking of ways to help Jan."

"We're not saying there is anything wrong with being single," Vivien said. "You know I loved being single. Now I love being with Troy."

Heather hesitated. She was unsure she'd be able to see the ghosts if they were around. It was a strange feeling to doubt her abilities. There had been so many of them in the house, and she hadn't felt them.

Unless the ghosts had followed Jan there, which seemed to be a possibility.

"We want you to be happy," Lorna said, "and maybe stay open to the possibilities. Maybe that's how you help Jan by being there for her."

"I can be there for her and not date her father." Heather didn't want to talk about this.

Was she attracted to Martin? Yes. He was a handsome man.

Did she want to disrupt her life? No. She worked hard to find her normal.

Did she get lonely sometimes and wish there was someone to hold her at night? Sure. Sometimes.

Did Martin have the kind of arms that looked like they could hold a woman close before he leaned over and kissed her? Well, damn Vivien anyway for even putting thoughts of sex into her head.

Heather gathered the four candles and set them together on the floor before bundling up the book. She shoved everything into the messenger bag.

"I'm sorry if we upset you," Lorna said.

"You didn't upset me." Heather stood with the messenger bag. "But if you want to help me, hand me a cupcake for the drive home."

CHAPTER EIGHT

WHEN A PHONE RANG in the middle of the night, it was never good news.

An instant knot formed in Heather's stomach before she became fully awake to the sound. A thousand panicked tragedies tried to run through her brain in the mere seconds it took her to fumble around in the dark looking for her phone—her mother, her brother, Vivien, Lorna, Mr. Willis, the theater, problem at one of the properties, fire at Anderson House as predicted in Jan's drawing.

After saying goodnight to her friends, Heather had come home to her empty house. She'd been preoccupied and forgot to plug in her cellphone, so it wasn't on her nightstand. She fumbled her way toward the sound, finally feeling her purse in the

---

dark. The blackout curtains made it impossible to see as they blocked out the moonlight. When she opened her purse, the light from the screen made it easier to see so she could check who was calling.

Unknown.

"Hello?" Heather sat on her bedroom floor and held the phone to her ear. Static pops answered. "Hello?"

The call disconnected.

Heather pulled the phone away and looked at the screen. It didn't give her any answers.

She pushed up from the floor and used the phone screen to light the way back to the bed. It was too late to call and check on people over a middle of the night misdial. She found her charger and plugged the phone in before crawling beneath the covers.

Heather waited, listening to see if anyone would call back before letting herself succumb to sleep. Just as she was about to drift off, the phone rang again, causing her to jolt awake. She rolled over and grabbed the phone.

Unknown.

"Hello?" Heather held the phone to her ear as she sat up in bed. Again static filled the earpiece speaker. "Hello? Is someone there? I can't hear you."

The static continued, a droning of white noise.

She thought she heard what could have been someone talking beneath the sissing, but it was too difficult to make out.

"I'm going to hang up," Heather said, waiting a few seconds longer. "If this is important, please find another phone and call back."

She set the phone down on the mattress next to her and laid on her side, watching it. Fifteen minutes passed. Nothing.

Heather closed her eyes, determined to go back to sleep.

Just as she relaxed, the phone rang again.

Heather sighed in irritation and answered. "Hello."

This time the line was silent.

"Hello? I can't hear you." Heather waited a few seconds before hanging up.

The phone rang again as she set it down on the mattress before she could even release it from her fingers. Heather instantly lifted it.

Unknown.

She answered and said nothing for several seconds. White noise static came from the earpiece.

"This isn't funny," she stated. "I'm trying to sleep."

She hung up.

It instantly rang again.

"What?"

Static pops covered what could have been a voice.

"Find a different phone or stop calling."

She hung up again and toggled volume off to mute the ring. Guilt tried to slip in that maybe it was something important. Maybe her mother was in the hospital, or Lorna was being attacked by demons again.

Heather lifted the phone and called Vivien.

"Mm?" Vivien's sleepy voice answered.

"Everything okay over there with you and Lorna?" Heather asked.

"I've got a little kink in my neck from laying on the pillow wrong," Vivien said, "and you interrupted a very nice dream with that cute actor from that movie with the thing?"

"Sword?" Heather guessed.

"No."

"Car?"

"No. Sexier than the car guy."

"Hey, I'm right here," Troy's voice came from behind Vivien's.

"No, it wasn't you," Vivien said.

"Ray gun?" Heather asked.

"Yeah, that guy," Vivien said. "He was making me a soufflé, but the zombie groaning made it fall."

"Okay, then," Heather chuckled. She stared at the ceiling, not really seeing it in the darkness. "What about Lorna?"

"She wasn't there," Vivien said, yawning. "She should be in her own dream."

"So, it's all good?"

"Why are you calling?" Vivien asked. "Yeah, everything is fine. William came over, and they're sleeping."

William was there. That meant it wasn't something to do with their mother. Bonnie would have called him first.

"I had a few staticky phone calls. I wanted to make sure it wasn't anything important," Heather said. "Go back to sleep. Sorry I woke you."

"Did you feel threatened?" Vivien asked. "Do you want us to come over there?"

Heather closed her eyes. "No. I'm going back to sleep."

"Night, love," Vivien said.

"Night." Heather hung up the phone and dropped it on the bed next to her.

The mattress began to vibrate as someone called the phone. Heather let loose an aggravated sigh. She pushed up on the bed and looked at the screen.

Unknown.

"Fuck you, unknown," she muttered. Still she found herself pushing the button and answering, "Hello."

She wasn't surprised by the static on the other end.

Heather stomped in anger to her bedroom door and opened it. She threw the phone toward the living room before shutting the door with a decisive thud. Let them call. She was done.

CHAPTER NINE

HEATHER TOUCHED her son's bedroom door lightly as she left the bathroom. Instead of passing by like she usually did, she reached for the doorknob and held it. Her fingers shook so severely that she barely felt the metal against her palm.

She pulled her hand away, but in the process, she must have turned the knob. The door inched open a crack. She stared into the dimly lit room to the unmade bed with the dark blue bedspread.

Heather brushed the back of her fingers against the door, edging it open slowly. Her son had picked the light blue shade of the walls to match a sports team. They'd painted it together.

The corner of a poster had detached from the

MICHELLE M. PILLOW

wall and curled forward to cover part of a football player. Toys sat on the floor where they'd been dropped to rest—a football, an action figure, and a slingshot. Everything was as her son left it.

Heather reached for the light switch, surprised when the light bulb turned on after being dormant for so long. Life had stopped in the room, and time had settled over it in a thin veil. Under the light, the layer of dust became obvious, having settled like desert sand swallowing an ancient city. Even the air had lost all smells, save the stale musk of a mausoleum. The grief first tickled her nose, burning as tears entered her eyes. She didn't let them fall but held them as suspended as the shrine before her.

Memories echoed through her mind. They came in a jumbled mess—laughter, tears, shouts of play, words of anger, threats of running away that were hardly meant and never acted upon. The floor and walls radiated with pain as the room waited for someone who would never return. It pulsed through the air, forming an invisible barrier over the door. It prickled her hand when she reached for the switch to shut off the light.

Heather closed the door, letting it latch before laying her hand against the wood. She wasn't sure

134

why today was the day she'd decided to peek inside. A heavy weight settled on her shoulders, and a dull ache centered over her chest.

The tips of her fingers pulsed from being pressed down. There was no need to whisper all the things she felt.

I love you.

I miss you.

I'm sorry.

I wish it were me instead of you.

I'm so tired.

I miss you so much, sweet boy.

Heather dropped her hands and walked away. It would be too easy to fall to the floor and sit by the door all day. She'd done it before, and it was difficult to lift herself back up when she succumbed to that depression.

Her cellphone was on the living room floor. She picked it up on her way toward the front door. A low battery warning appeared on the screen, and when she cleared it, she had a notification for eighty-seven missed calls.

"Seriously?" Heather shook her head. Some pranksters had way too much time on their hands.

The screen went black as it ran out of power.

Heather grabbed her notepad and keys off the end table on her way out the door. Even after she'd managed to fall back to sleep, she kept waking up, thinking she heard the phone ringing. The sound had invaded her dreams. It seemed she'd been starting a lot of her days under a veil of exhaustion lately.

Task by task, that is how she was going to live her day. She had her list of things that needed to be done, and she would add items to it, line by line until this notepad was full, and then she would get another and start filling that one up. It might sound stupid to some, but this habit was what kept her moving forward during her roughest of days. It motivated her to get out of bed and gave her direction when she didn't know what to do.

Unfortunately, this was one of those days that included waiting in line to renew her vehicle registration, a dental cleaning, and a surprise inspection at the home of one of her least favorite renters because the city had sent her a notice of car parts in the front yard. The renter on the original agreement was a meek woman, but she'd let her three grown sons move in with her after about three months living in the house. Since then, Heather received city complaints about every other month. How could she convince a mother to kick out her sons? Heather didn't have it in her to try.

What she wouldn't give to demolish a wall with a sledgehammer instead.

Heather connected her phone to the car charger. For some reason, she found herself not following her list as she drove toward Anderson House. She parked along the curb as work trucks were already in the drive.

In the light of morning, the house didn't look like anything to fear. The timeworn structure stood tall and proud against the sky, its outline cutting the blue and white. The lawn needed Bobby's attention desperately. The uneven grass and overgrown hedges, combined with the old paint on the siding, made the property look sad and neglected. No wonder everyone thought it was haunted.

Turns out, for once, when it came to ghosts, everyone else had been right, and she had been wrong.

So many spirits.

How could she have missed them?

Heather got out of the car and slowly walked up the front steps. She heard the faint sound of work coming from inside underscored by classic rock music.

A feeling of apprehension came over her. She

was used to the prickling feeling of a ghost nearby, but this was different. For the first time in her life, she didn't trust her abilities as a medium. Even now there could be an army of spirits around her, and she wouldn't know it. Like the other times she'd come to the house, she didn't feel an otherworldly presence.

There was another option. The ghosts could have followed Jan like they followed Heather around, though Heather should still be able to sense them around the girl.

She looked for Martin's truck but didn't see it. Heather could hardly blame the man if he decided to cancel the job. As a boss, she hoped not. He was damned good at his job. As a woman...well, damn Vivien and Lorna again for putting those thoughts into her head.

Maybe she should call him.

Maybe she should check on Jan.

Maybe she should mind her own damned business. If they wanted her help, they'd ask for it. How would she have felt if someone tried to interfere with her parenting decisions?

Walking into the home was more to prove to herself she wasn't scared than any real need to check on the job site. As she arrived on the second story, her gaze instantly went to the floor and then around the landing. They had summoned so many ghosts, and not all of them had left this plane of existence. Music came from upstairs.

Heather went up to the third story. Thomas had finished mudding the drywall. Dark spots along the seams told her it was still drying. He laid on his back on the floor, staring up at the ceiling while he sang softly with the radio.

"Break time?" Heather asked, startling him as he scrambled to sit up.

"Oh, hey." Thomas glanced guiltily around as if making sure he didn't leave anything unfinished. "Yeah, the guys are picking up more supplies."

"This wall looks great. You can't even tell there was water damage," Heather said, running her hand beneath a window. "Any issues with the house today I should know about?"

"Issues?" Thomas repeated. "Like what?"

"Plumbing noises, flickering lights, drafts," she bit the inside of her lip, trying to sound nonchalant, "ghosts?"

Thomas laughed, not taking her seriously. "I haven't seen any floating sheets or heard rattling chains, so I think we're good there."

Of course his image of a ghost came from an old cartoon.

"Martin mentioned that he'd be turning off the main power some time this week to install a new circuit breaker box," Thomas said.

"Have you heard from Martin today?" Heather asked, wondering if she needed to find a new electrician to take over. She wouldn't blame him if he never wanted to talk to her again after she butted in with his daughter.

Thomas shook his head in denial. "Not this morning. Probably had to pick up some wire. I'm sure he'll be in."

Heather went to look at the progress made in the third story rooms. The new bathroom was ready for finish work. Before there had not been water on the third floor.

"You know," Thomas said when she came back. "I had a great idea. While Martin's rewiring, we could install a home stereo system before the city officially makes this a historical landmark. Then it will be too late to change. You'd hardly notice the speakers in the ceiling."

"Have I ever said yes to that idea?" she asked. "And before you suggest it, I don't want a smart house, central vacuum, or a saltwater fish tank wall. The more techie stuff you put into a place, the more that can go wrong. The goal is to keep it simple."

"Your loss." Thomas pushed himself to his feet.

"What do you mean multiple problems?" Martin's voice came from below.

Heather checked the stairwell.

"So you're telling me someone tampered with my battery cables, and a fuse, and cut wires?" Martin sounded frustrated. She couldn't hear the answer, and it became clear he spoke on the phone. "No, I didn't file a police report."

She watched as his legs paced past the open stairwell.

"No, I didn't piss off a girlfriend," he stated.

His legs came back, and he stopped where she could see them.

"No, I didn't piss off anyone," Martin insisted.

"Dude, that's rough," Thomas said under his breath behind her as he eavesdropped as well.

"And your mechanic thinks they put antifreeze in the gas tank," Martin said before muttering, "Sure, why not?"

Heather heard him sigh in frustration as his weight shifted.

"Yes. Please call me when you have the estimate. Thanks." Martin's phone hand dropped by his thigh.

She instantly took a step back so he wouldn't catch her hovering.

Martin came up the stairs.

"Man, what the hell happened to your truck?" Thomas asked.

"I don't know. Teenagers were messing around, probably." Martin didn't sound convinced. "It wouldn't start this morning. When I tested the battery, it said it had a charge."

"Are you going to report it?" Thomas asked.

Martin's eyes met Heather's as he realized she was standing there. "Uh, probably, later, not much they can do, and my crap insurance probably won't cover it."

Heather watched Martin, not saying anything.

"Let me know if you need rides," Thomas said.

"Thanks," Martin answered. To Heather, he said, "Can I talk to you a minute?"

"Of course." Heather watched him expectantly.

He gestured that she join him in the other room.

"I'm going for coffee," Thomas announced. "I'll bring you some. Sounds like you could use a triple shot today."

"Thanks," Martin called after him. When they heard his steps descending, he said, "I wanted to make sure you were still all right with Jan being here. I told her to wait downstairs on the steps for me. I saw your car out front and wanted to check first."

Heather had not been expecting that question. "Yeah, of course. Nothing's changed."

"I wouldn't say that's entirely true." Martin crossed his arms before dropping them to his sides. He appeared uncomfortable as he shifted his weight. "I know you were trying to be kind to us, and I wanted to thank you for that."

"Okay...?" Heather tilted her head as she thought of his words. Was he glossing over what happened? "I mean, yes, I was trying to be kind, but I also want to help Jan."

"Thank you," Martin said. He pulled a hair tie from his pocket. He shifted again, running his hands through his hair before pulling it back. "This thing with my truck won't affect my work, but I might have to borrow Thomas to pick up some supplies later."

"You don't think it was teenagers, do you?" Heather heard the sound of a truck engine and became aware of how alone they were with Thomas gone. There would be more workers downstairs, somewhere, but they had no reason to venture up to the third floor.

"No, I don't." Martin went to where he'd cut an access hole into the wall and ran his finger along the edge, gently pulling at the opening as if to test it. "I know January's different from other kids and can be

143

very convincing. Ever since I can remember, she's always known things she shouldn't—like words she shouldn't know and how to do things."

"You think your ten-year-old daughter disabled your truck?" Heather asked.

"I'm pretty sure she did," Martin answered. "The doctor told me she was an observant child and probably picked up things in passing conversations or on television. He told me to limit her watching and monitor her reading."

"What kinds of things?" Heather asked.

"She'd talk about needing my toothbrush to clean her pretend Civil War relics so not to damage the patina," Martin said.

"Sounds like something that might be mentioned in a war documentary," Heather said.

"She was four. I'm pretty sure Civil War archeology wasn't covered on Saturday morning cartoons. What four-year-old says words like patina? Or Kafkaesque? Or T-square configuration? Or that's bloody brilliant?" He stopped pulling at the wall. "She baked a cake when she was five, from scratch. I had to keep the oven unplugged after that. A year later, she repaired an old radio with parts from the toaster, then repaired the toaster with parts from the coffee maker. I've lived through science experiments and hunger strikes and her correcting her teachers to the point they kept sending her to the principal's office so they wouldn't have to deal with her."

Heather knew instantly what had probably happened. "That's because she's getting answers from ghosts."

Martin frowned at her.

"I meant what I said last night to your daughter. I don't expect you to take my word for it and believe me, but you should believe her," Heather said. "You should believe what you, yourself, have said you've witnessed. How else would a five-year-old know how to combine ingredients the right way if she'd never been shown? Or how radios work? Someone must have taught her, someone who knew how to do those things. I know because they used to teach me how to do things, too. I think they liked having a kid who could see them and who they could impart knowledge on, or, yes, convince to get into trouble like some imaginary friend from hell—not literal hell, but you know what I mean. When I was seven, I had the spirit of a frat boy telling me to put plastic wrap around the toilet beneath the seat. The prank didn't end well for me, but he thought it was hilarious."

"There has to be another logical explanation," Martin insisted.

"Sure." Heather threw up her hands, and said sarcastically, "Your daughter is insane. I'm insane. Vivien and Lorna and my brother are insane. My grandmother was insane. Ghosts aren't real because that would be too hard to accept, and spirits are scary."

"You're mad." Martin softened his voice.

"No, I'm irritated, and hurt, and tired, and my stupid phone kept me up all night." She rubbed the back of her neck and closed her eyes. "And I'm worried about your daughter because she doesn't have anyone to help her understand that what she is going through is real and that there are ways she can learn to control it."

"You're asking me to believe in ghosts," Martin stated.

"Yes. I'm asking you to believe without proof, without seeing..." She let her voice trail off as an idea struck her. "No."

"No, you're not trying to get me to believe in ghosts?"

"No, I mean, I think we can show you proof," Heather said. "It worked with my brother. He used to think we were all crazy too, but then he saw for himself."

"How?" Martin didn't seem sure.

"I want you to join my friends and me for a séance," Heather said. "Tonight. At Warrick Theater. It'll be perfect. We have nothing on the schedule for tonight, so it will be empty."

Martin made a strange noise and shook his head. "I don't think that's a good idea."

"I don't think you can say no," Heather countered. "If there is a chance you can learn the truth about your daughter, don't you have to take it?"

He again shook his head in denial. "I—"

"If nothing happens, what harm is there?" she asked. "You'll be able to tell the story of how the strange lady who hired you to rewire a house convinced you to play séance one night. I'm sure your friends will find it amusing."

"I would never make fun of you to my friends," he said.

"Just say you'll join us tonight. What do you have to lose?"

"Besides my sanity?" He took a deep breath and held it. "Nothing, I guess. Sure, fine, but I don't want Jan involved with this."

Heather refrained from pointing out that his daughter was already highly involved. "My brother William is great with kids. He can take her for pizza and let her play the arcade games there. He'll have a cellphone if you want to check in with him."

"I..." He rubbed his temples before finishing. "I should get to work."

"I'll call my friends and set everything up." Heather knew she was being pushy, but she truly believed it was for the best. "I'll text you with the details."

Martin nodded. "Would you mind sending Jan up on your way out so I can keep an eye on her?"

Heather agreed as she left him alone. Already she knew Lorna and Vivien would say yes to her plan to help Jan. Vivien would claim this counted as Heather and Martin's first date, so she'd be extra eager to make sure things went well.

As Heather neared the first floor, she saw Jan sitting on the steps with a book. "Hey, there, good to see you again."

Jan glanced up at her but didn't stand. "I'm not supposed to talk to anyone."

"I understand," Heather said. "Your dad asked that I send you up to join him."

Jan stood and made a move to do just that.

"Wait, Jan, can I ask?" Heather looked around them for spirits. "Do you see any ghosts around us right now?"

Jan shook her head in denial. "You scared them last night when you sent some of them away. They don't want to come here anymore."

Jan ran up the stairs, her feet pounding loudly.

CHAPTER TEN
WARRICK THEATER

"HEATHER, seriously, what do I know about preteen girls?" William whispered as he grabbed his sister's arm. He kept her from joining Lorna and Vivien in the auditorium where they were setting up for the night's séance. He walked with her toward the concession and grabbed a box of candy out of the display. "I should be here with you where I can help."

Heather loved her brother, dearly, but sometimes he could be a bit of a dramatic. It was a quality he inherited from their mother—though he wasn't nearly as bad as her. Like Heather, he looked like a combination of their parents, though he'd gotten green eyes from the Stable side, and she'd inherited the Warrick brown. People usually accused him of being too quiet and wished he'd talk more. Heather never had that problem with him. If anything, she couldn't get him to shut up.

"What are people going to think if I suddenly show up in town with a kid?" he insisted.

"That you kidnapped her," Heather answered wryly. "Obviously."

"You're not funny." He paced to the front glass doors of the lobby and frowned. "Do you think this is a good idea? This Martin guy is an outsider. Troy doesn't even do séances with the three of you, and he's dating Viv."

"That's because Troy didn't need convincing to believe that spirits are real. He believed Vivien when she told him." Heather gave him a pointed look as she silently added, *unlike some people I know.*

William had needed to see to believe, even though when he'd been really young, he'd had some experiences that were written off as imaginary friends. They had gone away, and her brother had spent his life denying their family's legacy. He'd hated it when people mentioned it. Though he'd gotten better and he was trying to be supportive, she noticed he sometimes fell back on old habits. It was difficult for him to talk about ghosts with people outside of their trusted circle.

"I'm sorry for not believing you and for all the shit I gave you growing up about it," William said.

Heather could sense he was sorry for a lot of things she wouldn't let him say. She didn't need magic or a ring to tell her that much. She knew her brother.

The inability to speak freely about their feelings was one trait they had in common. They both kept their emotions close and didn't speak of them often. Though William had been blessed with an expressive face so people often took his quiet in stride. They tended to think Heather was just a bitch because apparently her expression didn't reveal what she was thinking. "If we had been a normal family, you would have given me shit about something else. It's what siblings do."

William nodded, accepting her answer before changing the subject back. "Why can't Troy babysit the girl?"

"I'm going to need you to man up here, bro." Heather patted his shoulder a couple of times. "Troy can't do it because he's not you."

"Why does he have to be me?" William arched a brow. "It's not like I know anything about boy bands and lip gloss."

"Wow, yes, because that's what all preteen girls are into," Heather drawled.

"What? See, I told you. I don't know. What does this kid even like?"

"Construction sites and pizza," Heather answered.

"I know about construction sites," William said, more as if to himself than her.

"I'd hope so since that's your job." Heather laughed. "See, you'll be fine. Just take her for pizza and don't come back until I call you. If anyone asks, just tell them you have an illegitimate daughter from a one night stand."

"You're still not funny."

"Debatable," Heather teased.

"Why did you say that it needs to be me who babysits her? There are like a million high school girls looking for that kind of work. What are you not telling me?" He crossed his arms over his chest and tried to look stern.

"Because Jan is like I was." Heather met her brother's gaze. "She sees spirits everywhere, Will, just like I did. No, worse than I did because she didn't have a grandma Julia to help her understand that not all ghosts are her friends. They're not all bad, but the ones who don't move on usually have some kind of damage in their souls—tragedy or pain or confusion, or something they did that keeps them from wanting to move on to face a final judgment. They latch onto her, influencing her."

Heather took a deep breath, knowing she could make her brother understand.

"She's been going at it alone," she continued. "That's why I need to convince Martin that what his daughter is going through is real. He's a good man and a great father, but he's at his wit's end. He's homeschooling her with online classes. I know it looks like she's thriving, but that isolation is only cementing these spirit friendships. Trust me. If I had not met Vivien and made a friend in middle school, I would have been that weird old lady wandering around talking to herself that parents shy their kids away from."

"You are a weird old lady that parents shy their kids away from," William answered, feigning seriousness.

Heather scrunched up her face but ignored the brotherly jibe. "I need you to do this because she'll be comfortable around you. She is used to construction-types after being raised by a single father around job sites. Also, because you're not going to get freaked out if she starts talking to someone who isn't there or looks like she can't concentrate because a ghost is chattering in her ear. You went through it with me. You'll be perfect with her."

"I was terrible to you when you were her age," he said.

"You're the only one I trust who can do this."

William nodded. "Since you put it like that. Yeah, of course."

"Thank you." Heather sighed with relief.

"Poor Jan," William said. "She's lucky to have found you. If anyone can help her, it's you."

"I hope so." Heather wasn't so sure. She'd been trying to think of what advice Julia had told her as a child to make her feel better. It hadn't been words exactly, but a feeling of acceptance and a grandmother's love. If she wanted to give that same feeling to Jan, she needed to help her father understand what was real.

"So this Martin guy? Anything you want to tell me? Viv says that you're—" William began.

"And this conversation is finished," Heather cut him off.

William laughed. "I see Vivien knows what she's talking about, per usual. You're blushing." In a singsong voice, he taunted, "Heather has a boyfriend. Heather has a—"

"Shut up." Heather strode away from him.

"He better treat you right, or I'm going to have a talk with him," William stated.

Heather walked faster, not dignifying that with a response.

"I love you, sis," he called after her.

"Yeah, yeah, I love you too," she answered.

Lorna and Vivien had set up a card table on the stage with four chairs. The cloth, candles, and book were already placed on top of it. She noticed Lorna had brought the food bag with her so they'd have sugary snacks to replenish with afterward. It was a big step up from being on the floor. Heather was glad. In recent years, her back had begun to protest sitting on the hard surfaces.

Summoning Julia seemed like the safest bet. She would be able to answer any of Martin's questions and wouldn't pose a threat. Plus, she was already a strong spirit and wouldn't be hard to call forth from the great beyond.

"I was just telling Vivien I think we need to rethink this cloth," Lorna said as Heather came down the aisle toward the stage.

Heather glanced to where Julia often manifested but didn't see the ghost. "Why's that?"

"It didn't work to contain the spirits last night,"

Lorna ran her hands over the cloth, smoothing it down.

"It doesn't work on Julia, either," Vivien said. When they'd séanced Julia so everyone could see her, her grandmother had manifested outside of the circle. She'd actually possessed Vivien's body for a short while, making her dance burlesque.

"Julia?" Heather called out to the spirit. "Can you show yourself to me, please? I need to talk to you."

She looked around, but Julia didn't appear.

"It's important," Heather insisted. "We're going to try to introduce you to someone tonight. I need you to behave and take it easy on him. He's new to all of this, but he needs our help."

Still, no sign of her.

"You always said if we could help a neighbor, we should," Heather insisted. "He has a daughter who is like us. We need to help her."

"Where is she?" William had pushed the velvet curtain aside and looked in. He glanced toward the wall to hook it back, but the curtain holdback was broken and she needed to replace it.

"I don't know," Heather answered with a shrug. "I don't see her anywhere."

William glanced around, but he wouldn't be able

to see their grandma either. "I need coffee. You want?"

Heather nodded. "Yes, please."

"Coffee?" William yelled so the other two would hear him.

"Latte, thank you, baby," Lorna answered.

"Cappuccino extra shot," Vivien called.

"On it!" William ducked back out.

"Last night was..." Heather shook her head as she walked toward the front of the auditorium. She didn't need to say it. Last night had been a surprise. It was evident that there had been too many ghosts, and they'd essentially busted out of the circle. They had done a handful of séances, so it's not like they were experts by any stretch of the imagination.

"I've been worried about Jan," Lorna said. "Do you think anything negative came over, like with Glenn?"

"It felt different," Vivien assured her. "I thought the sensation I experienced with Glenn was because he was a jerk, but there had to be jerks there last night and it was nothing like that first time. Last night felt like a crowded bus station—a bunch of people with no choice but to be there, but also in a hurry to leave."

"William has agreed to babysit her while we do

this. Making Martin aware of the supernatural will better equip him to help his daughter if anything does happen." Heather went up the stairs and peered at the stage. Examining the properties was a habit that her mind couldn't break as she looked for mars and chips in the black floor paint. She didn't find any.

"He'll do a good job," Lorna said.

"So, what kind of treat did you make for us tonight?" Heather asked, nodding at the food bag.

Lorna gave a tiny laugh.

"What?"

"I didn't bake this time," Lorna said.

"That's fine," Heather said. "Did you grab something from the bakery?"

"Not exactly." Lorna covered her mouth.

"What am I missing?" Heather asked Vivien.

"I baked," Vivien said. "Chocolate cake."

"She insisted," Lorna said.

"I wanted to help." Vivien grinned.

"You did help," Lorna said. "I'm sure it tastes great."

Curious, Heather went to check the bag. She pulled out a glass cake pan and lifted the blue silicone lid. Specks of brown crumbs had been dragged through the white frosting to create the effect of muddy snow, and there was a divot in the center.

"Did you drop something on it?" Heather asked, trying not to laugh.

"Maybe," Vivien mumbled.

"Now you have to tell me," Heather said.

"I was reaching for a toothpick to make sure it was baked all the way, and a bottle of maple syrup fell from the top cabinet," Vivien explained.

"Did syrup get into the cake?" Heather asked. "That might taste all right."

"No. The bottle just bounced and then fell on the floor when I tried to catch it. The glass broke, and syrupy shards went everywhere. Since I was barefoot, I had to yell for Troy to bring me a paper towel. By the time we got everything cleaned up, I was over the whole baking thing, and so I just dumped some frosting on it—"

"While it was still warm, thus the crumbs," Lorna inserted.

"—and called it good," Vivien finished.

"I'm sure it tastes great," Lorna said.

"You said that already," Vivien answered.

"Well, that's all that matters." Lorna smiled.

"I feel like you just patted me on the head." Vivien laughed.

Heather watched the two of them, almost jealous

of the roommate fun they'd had over the simple baking of a cake.

Lorna's smile fell. "What is it, Heather?"

Heather had not meant for her friends to pick up on her feelings. It was a fleeting pang that didn't warrant a discussion.

"Nothing." She waved her hand in dismissal.

Lorna and Vivien tried reaching for her to read her emotions for themselves.

Heather stepped back before they could grab hold of her. "I'm fine. I swear. I was just thinking of Lorna's roommate idea. It might be kind of fun, but the logistics of it are—"

"I'm in," Lorna stated.

"Me too," Vivien added instantly. "Pick which house you want to live in."

"Old Anderson House," Lorna said without missing a beat.

"Not you. Heather pick," Vivien corrected.

Heather thought of her home, of her son's closed bedroom door that she touched every day. She didn't think she was capable of leaving.

"It's okay. You think about it," Vivien said, reading Heather's wave of pain even without physical contact. "No pressure."

"We love you," Lorna said. "Viv is right. No pressure."

"We can talk about this later," Heather said. "Right now, we need to concentrate on easing Martin into the supernatural world and making him understand that ghosts are real."

"Ease?" Vivien shook her head. "I don't think there is such a thing when it comes to this. I think all we can do is throw him in the deep end without a life preserver and hope he can swim."

CHAPTER ELEVEN

HEATHER STOOD in the lobby with Martin as they watched William's truck leave. She put her hand on his arm, letting her ring finger touch him. She felt his hesitance to let Jan go. She couldn't blame him for that. But she also felt his desperation for answers. This was a man who had tried everything he could to help his daughter. He took her to doctors, pastors, and a priest. He stayed up endless nights watching over her as she slept, trying to figure out what was happening to her.

The knowledge came to her, not like a vision, but as an impression. Heather could picture herself in his place, doing all of those things.

Helpless.

Desperate.

MICHELLE M. PILLOW

Alone.

She withdrew her hand. "It's been so difficult for you. All those doctors. All that worry."

His expression registered surprise.

"We're here to help you now," she said. "I promise. We can help."

"I don't know what to believe." He leaned toward the door to look down the street. William's taillights had disappeared. "But I'm out of options on how to help her. When I think of her fiddling with my truck, of all the ways she could have been hurt or even killed, I can't…"

Heather rubbed her hand along his back, attempting to comfort him. The touch felt intimate as she discovered the muscles along his spine, and she withdrew her hand. "I know. Thankfully she wasn't."

"It's not just the truck, Heather." Martin turned to face her. "She finds ways to sneak out of the house. What am I supposed to do? Bolt her in her room each night? Chain her to me so she's never out of my sight? I don't want that. I want to be a good father. I want to keep her safe. I want her to be happy and grow up normal and not talking to people who aren't there. I want to be able to send her to school without worrying that she'll start a dice game during recess."

Normal. The word stung.

Heather slowly nodded. "I understand."

It was true. She did understand, but that didn't mean the word didn't hurt. How many times in her life had she been made to feel peculiar or weird? If it were just about her, she'd have let the comment go.

"What your daughter and I can do might not be what you want for her, but that doesn't make her abnormal." Heather took a step away from him. He was standing too close, and the smell of his cologne made it hard to concentrate. "If you want her to be safe, she needs to be able to trust you, talk to you."

"I want her to trust me and talk to me," Martin said.

"Then she needs to know you believe her." Heather paced away from him in aggravation. A ghost appeared near the concessions to watch them. The woman had died in the fifties. She manifested sometimes but never said anything. Heather frowned at her. "Go away."

"What? But I thought we were...?" Martin appeared confused.

"Not you." Heather frowned, gesturing to the ghost only to find she'd disappeared. "Never mind."

"Is this what was happening the other day when we were going over the wiring? You weren't yelling at me. Did you think someone was there with us? Talking to you?"

Heather didn't answer. "This séance will work best in the auditorium."

"Séance," he repeated as if testing how the word felt in his mouth.

"Yes. We are going to summon the spirit of my grandmother, Julia Warrick," Heather said, leading the way toward where they set up on the stage.

"Warrick? Like the name on the plaque outside?" Martin followed her.

"Yes. My maiden name is Warrick. Grandma Julia was a brilliant businesswoman. She commissioned the construction of this and several other buildings in town, most notably this theater and a hotel. The hotel burned down." Heather held the velvet curtain away from the door leading toward the seats so that he could pass through. "This theater was her favorite. For years she held séances here. People would come from all around to speak to their loved ones through Julia. She was a trusted medium and spiritualist."

Martin didn't speak, though it looked like he had several disbelieving things to stay.

"Aside from her work as a medium, she danced burlesque for a time, was a known bootlegger during

Prohibition, a pot farmer, wrote a recipe column for the local paper and had a small stint playing piano in clubs for a jazz singer." Heather smiled with pride. "She was a remarkable woman."

"It sounds like it," Martin agreed.

"Martin, hello," Lorna greeted from the stage. "It's good to see you again."

He nodded. "Hello."

"Lorna," Lorna pointed at herself. She sat in one of the chairs with the séance book open on her lap, copying over one of the séance incantations.

"Yes, I remember." Martin looked toward Vivien. "Hello."

"Hi," Vivien called to him.

"Thank you for your desire to help my daughter," Martin said to all of them. "I appreciate what you are trying to do here, but I have to tell you upfront I don't believe in this kind of thing. I won't mock you for your beliefs, but I just have to be honest."

"Thank you for your honesty." Vivien gave a little smile. "We tend to find seeing is believing for most people."

Heather tried not to laugh. Vivien made it sound like they did this kind of thing often.

Martin climbed onto the stage and looked at the ceiling before inspecting the area.

"There are no trick wires or mirrors or projectors," Vivien said. "Feel free to check whatever you like."

"That's not true. We have the movie projector," Lorna corrected.

"Which will only prove helpful if we decide to screen Casablanca later," Vivien answered. "Inspect anything you want. We have nothing to hide," Vivien said.

Martin lifted the cloth from where it draped over the edge of the table and looked underneath. He picked up each chair and rocked them to test their stability. Then he paced along the back of the stage to check out what was hidden behind there.

"Satisfied?" Heather asked.

"Yes." Martin turned to the table. "So how does this work? Do we turn off the lights, light some candles? Put our hand on a Ouija board? Gaze into a crystal ball?"

"Not quite." Lorna closed the book and set it in the middle of the table. She held onto the piece of paper she'd been writing on. "It's incantations."

Martin studied the book cover and lightly lifted a corner with his index finger to peek inside at the title page that read, "*Warrick.*"

Vivien pulled a lighter out of her pocket and held it. "Say it."

He glanced up at her.

"Say what? Warrick?" He pulled his hand away, and the cover dropped.

"Not that. Say what you're thinking. You're worried we're doing something satanic," Vivien stated.

"I wasn't going to say that." Martin shook his head.

"But you're thinking it." Vivien gave him a soft smile. "It's all right to be nervous. We don't worship Satan, or sacrifice things, or make pacts with the devil."

"But we believe there is a devil," Lorna said. "And a God."

It was a little hard not to believe in something more when they talked to ghosts and had summoned a demon from another dimension.

"Think of what we do as magic, not good or bad, just magic," Vivien explained.

"I disagree," Heather put forth, coming to stand beside Martin. "I would say what we do is good magic, or at least what we try to do."

"What I mean is, this kind of magic is only as

good as the person wielding it," Vivien clarified. "And we mean to do good."

This was the first time they had to try to convince someone so their speeches weren't fine-tuned. Besides the three of them, only William and Troy knew the truth. William had grown up with supernatural talk thanks to the family legacy, so even for the many years he'd been a nonbeliever, he still knew about it. Troy was an academic and had accepted Vivien's abilities. He'd asked a lot of detailed questions about what they do, so his prompts had kept them from having to explain something that was hard for most people to comprehend in the abstract.

"Think of it as biological evolution," Lorna suggested. "Like how humans, in general, have become taller over the last one hundred and fifty years, or how brains developed over human evolution. What we do is like that."

Heather knew what Lorna was trying to say but wasn't sure her point was getting across.

"So talking to the dead is evolution?" Martin asked, clearly not following where Lorna tried to lead.

"Let me try this again," Lorna said, glancing at Vivien and Heather for help. "We've evolved... You know, the explanation went better in my head. Never mind."

"I think I got this," Vivien took over. "For example, I have the ability to read people. My ancestors developed gifts other people didn't have. Just as some people grow tall and athletic to become great basketball players, my ancestors' minds grew strong, and they became fortune tellers. They passed that genetic trait down to me, and so now I'm clairsentient-claircognizant. I can sense things about people."

"So you're a mentalist," he reasoned. "You read microexpressions, things like that."

"I'd call it psychic," Vivien corrected before gesturing to Lorna. "Lorna's evolution is the ability to transfer energy. She can heal people."

Martin looked at Lorna in disbelief. "So then why not just go to the hospital and make people better? Why not cure Jan? Take all of this away from her?"

"Healing comes with a price," Lorna said. "It's not curing someone so much as giving their illness to someone else."

"And what Jan has doesn't need to be cured," Heather objected to the wording.

"Lorna is also very good at finding lost items," Vivien continued.

He looked at Heather as if expecting her to say something.

Part of her wanted him to know everything, to know her, the real her. Another part of her wanted to stop this conversation and reverse time to hide her true self. The latter was the more familiar territory. She took comfort in her secrets. But it was already way too late for that.

"You already know I talk to ghosts," she said. "I see and hear what other people can't."

"Ready?" Vivien asked the group.

Martin nodded.

Vivien lit one of the candles. All four wicks set fire at once. Martin made a strange noise and lifted one of the candles from the table to examine it.

"Figure it out?" Vivien asked.

"Trick candles?" He set it back down in its place.

"Magic," Vivien answered. "Pure and simple magic."

"I wouldn't say simple," Lorna protested, glancing up from the book.

"I have to agree with Lorna," Heather said. Nothing about their lives had been simple since they found Julia's rings.

Heather moved to sit across from Lorna. She

gestured to her right for Martin to sit next to them. Vivien took her place across from Martin's chair.

"So why the theater stage?" Martin asked as he slowly sat down.

"Like I mentioned before, this place was my grandma's favorite building. She likes to hang out here," Heather answered. "So the location means a lot to her. Also, this is where she used to hold her public séances back in the day, so it makes sense it would be an emotionally charged place for her to show herself to us."

Lorna placed a piece of paper on the table in front of Martin. "This is the incantation that you'll say with us."

He leaned over and read the words to himself.

Heather shared a looked with Vivien and Lorna. She could tell they were all thinking the same thing. They really hoped this worked. William was Julia's grandson, so it made sense she would show herself to him the last time they'd summoned her. Martin was a stranger. They had never tried this before.

Heather looked for her grandmother, hoping to find her so she could explain before they started. Julia was still nowhere to be found.

"Any questions?" Vivien asked Martin.

He shook his head in denial.

Heather reached out her hand. He glanced at it and hesitated before taking it. The warmth of his fingers closed around hers, and she felt the flow of his energy coming into her hand. It traveled up her arm and settled low in her stomach.

Wait, no. Crap. That wasn't the beginning of magic. That was pure sexual attraction.

His eyes stayed on hers as if he felt it too. His fingers moved slightly against her, a tiny caress that made her shiver. The prolonged contact caught her complete attention. She glanced at his mouth. All of the attraction she'd been trying to deny between them began to bubble to the surface. She started to lean in for a...

"*Uh-hem,*" Vivien cleared her throat.

Heather rapidly blinked as she came out of her daze.

Vivien held her hand toward her, not bothering to hide her smirk of amusement. Heather slowly reached out and joined hands with her. At the contact, her hair began to lift from her shoulders. She felt Vivien and Lorna's emotions mingling inside her as they connected.

When she turned her attention back to Martin, he'd joined hands with Lorna and was staring down at the piece of paper intently. The lights flickered and dimmed. The candles burned brighter.

Martin's eyes widened as they looked around the table at him. His longer hair started to lift, and he let go of Lorna to pat it down. The reaction appeared automatic, and he caught himself mid-pat. He looked at the three of them as if realizing their hair was doing it too. He returned his hand to Lorna's.

"Ready?" Lorna asked.

"Not really," Martin said under his breath.

"Just say the words with us and don't release hands until we tell you to," Heather said. "I promise it's going to be all right."

She hoped she wasn't lying.

"It might be scary at first, but Julia won't harm you," Vivien added.

Heather glanced at the spell Lorna had written out for Martin. It was a new addition to the book; one they'd modified and added from Julia's incantations. It had worked to bring Julia forth the last time, and they hadn't wanted to forget it.

She felt Martin's nervousness. He tried to hide it, but it was there.

"I feel strange," Martin whispered to Heather.

"That's normal," she said. "It's all part of the process. Try to relax, and don't forget to breathe."

He nodded, and she could see his skepticism was beginning to fade.

"As we say the words, concentrate on wanting to talk to Julia Warrick," Heather instructed.

He nodded again.

Their emotions continued to flow freely through her, coming from Martin's hand through her body and out to Vivien. The feelings mixed together as if they all became one in a spiritual sense. Lorna fretted about Jan and finding answers for Martin. Vivien appeared excited to be helping someone outside of their circle as if she just realized this might be their calling in life. Heather wasn't sure she agreed with Vivien on that point.

Heather worried about what Martin might learn about her in the process, but he appeared to be more confused and apprehensive about the sensation than anything else. He was also determined to help his daughter at any cost. That one fact was what kept him seated in his chair.

"Say the words," Heather instructed, prompting the others to say in unison, "Spirits tethered to this plane we humbly seek your guidance. Spirits search amongst your numbers for the spirit we seek. We call forth Julia Warrick from the great beyond."

Heather stared at the closed book as she waited to feel her grandma's presence.

After a long pause, Martin whispered, "Is that it?"

"Try again," Heather said. "Focus on calling Julia to us."

"Spirits tethered to this plane, we humbly seek your guidance," they repeated in unison. "Spirits search amongst your numbers for the spirit we seek. We call forth *Julia Warrick* from the great beyond."

Heather kept her hand on his as she turned to look at the auditorium. She felt the slightest hint of a presence but wasn't sure if it was her grandmother or someone else.

"Again," Vivien said.

Again, they repeated, "Spirits tethered to this plane we humbly seek your guidance. Spirits search amongst your numbers for the spirit we seek. We call forth Julia Warrick from the great beyond."

"Do you hear that?" Martin looked over his shoulder. Heather tightened her grip so he wouldn't let go.

"What? Does it sound like jazz?" Vivien asked. She gave Heather a meaningful look. "That's what I heard playing last time, before Julia..."

Vivien's eyes widened, and she didn't finish the

thought. It was what had been playing when Julia borrowed Vivien's body to dance. The rest of them had not heard it.

"Julia," Heather hurriedly said. "Don't."

Please don't wear Martin like a human suit and dance the hoochie-coochie, she silently pleaded.

"No, not music," Martin answered. "It's..."

Martin frowned, turning in his seat to look over his other shoulder.

"Do you hear anything?" Lorna asked Heather.

Heather shook her head. She felt a slight presence.

"I think someone is crying, or maybe moaning?" He shifted in his seat. "I feel like it's behind me. What is that?"

Did they bring forward a weepy ghost?

Heather looked over the empty stage. The overhead lights went completely out, casting them in darkness except for the candles. The ghoulish effect of the fiery glow flickered across their faces in harsh contrast.

"I don't like this," Martin said. His uneasiness intensified. Heather felt his panic building through the connection.

"Shh," Vivien whispered. "I think I see something."

Heather saw it too. A soft glow formed in the darkness. The image of a woman appeared like mist, the exact translucent shape lacking definition, yet the impression of a skirt and legs formed in white. As the image gained strength, the sound of moaning came with it. The ghostly woman stood with her back to them, her head down as if she cried into her hands.

"I hear it," Lorna said.

"Me too," Vivien answered.

"Who is it?" Lorna asked.

Heather felt their eyes glancing toward her for answers, but she didn't have one.

"Martin, do you recognize her?" Heather asked, wondering if maybe it was his dead wife since he'd heard her first.

"No," Martin said. She felt his hand tighten on hers.

The ghost began to rotate slowly, floating as her legs didn't move. The moaning became louder as the voice crackled. A pale impression of muted colors developed in the misty form. Dark lines formed over the ghost's skin like throbbing veins. Short dark hair fell forward to hide the face.

Heather's breath caught. She tried to remember the words they'd said to send the demon away, but her mind was blank. Fear crept through her, partly hers, partly her friends' as it came through their joined hands.

The ghost's head began to twitch as if finding it hard to move as her face lifted to look at them.

"Oh, shit," Lorna whispered.

Martin tensed.

"Is that...?" Vivien sounded confused.

The ghost quickly spun the rest of the way, lifting her hands. Her face contorted as she yelled, "Boo!"

The candleflames burst like fiery torches. Lorna let out a yelp. Heather's heart leaped in her chest and began to hammer violently. Martin ripped his hand from Heather's grasp as he positioned himself between the ghost and the three women. He put his arms wide as if to shield them from harm with his body.

"Stay behind me," Martin ordered.

"Julia?" Vivien asked.

Heather pressed her hand over her chest and tried to take a calming breath. Julia stood, shoulders hunched, breathing hard as her head twitched.

"Grandma?" Heather asked, attempting to push past Martin to get a better look.

He grabbed her as she tried to pass and pulled her against his chest. "Don't."

Heather stiffened in surprise at being held so close. His strong arms wrapped around her, and she didn't instantly fight to be free.

A snickering sounded, and they all stared at Julia. The ghost's color slowly improved, and the twitching became more of a shake. She looked like the younger version of herself, the jokester twenty-year-old who ran hooch across state lines. Her bobbed hair darkened and curled with finger waves. Red lipstick filled in her lips. Her tattered dress melted into a pair of high-waisted trousers and a blouse.

"Julia, what the hell?" Vivien demanded. "You scared the crap out of us."

Julia straightened her posture and began to full-on laugh. The lights flickered, coming back on. "You should have seen your faces. I couldn't resist."

Heather frowned. She pushed lightly against Martin so he'd release her. "It's fine. It's just my grandma."

Julia held out her hand, and a hat appeared. She used it to fan her face.

"That's your Grandma Julia?" Martin asked, standing close to Heather.

"In the flesh." Julia lifted her arms to the side and struck a pose.

"One version of her, anyway," Heather answered.

"And she's a..." He took an audible breath.

"Ghost," Vivien prompted. "Yes."

Martin took another deep breath. "Ghost."

"Well, former flesh," Julia continued, not really listening to them. She put the fedora on her head at a stylish angle. "Unless one of you ladies wants to give me a ride somewhere? Viv, doll face, how about it? Scooch over and let me in again."

"Stay out of Viv, Grandma," Heather warned. "We talked about that."

"You are such a fuddy-duddy," Julia dismissed, before scolding, "and I told you I hate when you call me that. Do I look like a grandma to you?"

"This is so..." Martin said under his breath. He held very still. Heather touched his arm, trying to reassure him. Julia was a lot to take in even when someone was used to ghosts.

"Uh, Heather, is he all right?" Lorna asked, going to his chair to turn it around the other way to face him. "Maybe he should sit down."

Julia turned her attention to Martin as if looking at him for the first time. "Oh my stars, you brought me a werewolf!"

"What?" Martin shook his head. "No. I—"

"*Aroooo*," Julia howled, throwing back her head. When she finished, she disappeared and then reappeared next to Martin. He jumped in surprise. "Hello, there, handsome. Aren't you just a burly slice of sexy?"

Vivien chuckled, and Julia glanced over to wink at her.

"Heather?" Martin held very still, as if afraid to move. Julia let her hand hover close to his cheek.

"Julia, leave the poor man alone," Heather ordered.

"Have you ever thought of piercing the veil?" Julia winked and somehow made the suggestion sound very, very dirty.

Vivien laughed harder, covering her mouth.

"Don't encourage her," Heather scolded.

"Sorry," Vivien said from beneath her fingers as she fought for control. Her shoulders shook a couple of times as the laughter trailed off.

"Well?" Julia insisted.

"I don't know what that..." Martin gave a slight shake of his head. "No, ma'am."

"Julia." Heather gave her grandma a pointed look. "Seriously, I need you to behave."

"You let me know if you change your mind, sugar pie. I'll bring you over to my side so you can see how the other half lives." Julia winked at him but backed off. She disappeared and reappeared next to Heather. "I told you a sexy man was entering your life. Was I right, or am I always right?"

"She was just teasing," Lorna said to Martin. "She's not threatening to hurt you."

He gave a half nod.

"Do you want to sit down?" Lorna asked him.

He didn't move.

"Julia, please, I need your help," Heather said.

Julia frowned and made a show of sighing and rolling her eyes. "Always with the help. You never call me to do anything fun. You finally bring a hot man around, and you won't even let me flirt with him a little."

"I'll introduce you to my boyfriend Troy," Vivien offered. "You can flirt with him all you want."

"Boyfriend? Do tell!" Julia focused her attention on Vivien.

"Sexy, funny, smart," Vivien answered.

"When can I meet him?" Julia waved her hand. "Ring him up. Get him over here."

Martin watched the interplay, not moving or making a sound. Heather couldn't tell if he was stunned or frightened.

"Are you all right?" Heather asked him.

"That's a ghost," Martin said.

"Yes." Heather nodded.

"I'm not a werewolf," he stated.

"I know," she said, thankful he wasn't freaking out too badly. "Werewolves are not real."

"Like hell they're not," Julia piped up.

"You need to stop trying to scare us," Heather insisted.

"Viv knows what I'm talking about, don't you, doll?" Julia chuckled. "Nothing wrong with a little hair on the chest when he's an animal in the sack, is there?"

"I'm sorry. Maybe we should have séanced someone a little less *Julia* for your first time," Heather said. Though she didn't know who else that might have been. "Are you all right? You're not saying anything or moving."

"It's not what I expected." Martin slowly flexed his hand, lifting it as to prove he could move. "I mean, I didn't actually expect to see a ghost, but if I had it wouldn't have been like this."

"You flatter me," Julia teased. She lifted her fingers and a long, skinny cigarette holder appeared with a lit cigarette on the end. Smoke curled into the air as she waved the holder to enunciate her words,

"Hey, Lorna, why are you being so quiet? Set a wedding date yet?"

"We're not engaged," Lorna said.

Heather had a feeling it was only a matter of time.

"You will be, though," Vivien assured her, having psychically predicted it when William and Lorna first got together.

"William wanted me to tell you hello, though," Lorna added.

"I don't want to be the one to tell you this," Julia disappeared and materialized beside Lorna, "but you're not getting any younger. Tick tock says the alarm. How am I supposed to be reincarnated if you don't get pregnant soon?"

Lorna touched her stomach and her mouth opened, but sound didn't come out.

Julia brushed her ghostly finger along Lorna's nose. "I'm joking. You all are so serious."

"Good, because I'm done having children. I've raised my three," Lorna stated. "This womb is closed for business."

"Did your grandmother die young?" Martin asked. "She's not very old."

"Julia's what we call an intelligent haunting. She's aware and can manipulate her surroundings,"

Heather said. "She has several incarnations. This one is 1920s Julia. She's exuberant, more so today than most."

"Exuberant?" Julia scoffed. Her cigarette disappeared. "Quit talking about me like I'm not here."

"Shh, the adults are having a conversation," Heather told her. Technically, in her forties, she was older than the current Julia.

Julia took off her hat and threw it at Heather. It disappeared before making contact. "Hey, *you* asked to see *me*. No need to be snippy."

"Julia, I love you, but I need my grandma," Heather said.

"Are you still worried about that demon?" Julia asked. "I told you before. You exorcised it."

Heather cringed. *Dammit.*

"Demon?" Martin demanded. "No one mentioned demons."

"Julia, please," Heather begged.

"Fine," Julia grumbled. "If it means that much to you."

"It does." Heather nodded.

Julia's image aged as they watched, shimmering as it changed. Gray streaks grew down her dark hair like rivers flowing to the tips. Her hips widened, and the patterns on her shirt became bolder. Trousers turned into a calf-length skirt. Every era of her grandma had been a stylish one, and this one was closer to the Julia that Heather remembered.

To see her grandma's face in its more familiar form caused Heather's heart to ache a little. She wanted to hug her so badly, but her arms would only fall into the cold chill of Julia's body.

When she spoke, the spirit's tone was less playful. "What is it, love?"

"What did she mean by demons?" Martin asked.

"She was joking," Vivien lied. "Ignore that."

"Grandma, I want to introduce you to my friend, Martin," Heather said. "He needed to meet you."

"Well, I'm flattered. It's been a while since I was tracked down by a fan," Julia said. "How do you do, Martin?"

"Fine, thank you, ma'am," Martin said.

"He's a polite one," Julia mused. She studied him for a moment. "You're not a fan, are you?"

He shook his head in denial. "No, ma'am, sorry."

"Then how can I help you?" Julia smiled. She didn't move around as much as before.

"It's my daughter, January," he answered. "She sees things."

"Spirits," Heather clarified. "Jan is like us."

"Is she a cousin?" Julia wondered. "I don't

remember a Jan in the family. Is her mother related to the Warrick family?"

"No. I don't think so," Martin said.

"Her mother died in childbirth," Heather explained. "Jan barely survived."

"Ah, I see now. She was born into the veil." Julia nodded. "I've heard stories. It's extremely rare. How old is she?"

"Ten," Martin said.

"She hasn't had anyone to teach her," Heather said. "Not like I had you."

Julia frowned and shook her head. "That poor creature. I'm not sure what I can do. How long has she been in the asylum? If she can see us, it won't be hard to get a message to her."

"She's not in a psychiatric facility," Martin said. "She lives with me."

"But you're not a medium," Julia dismissed.

"No," Martin agreed.

"And she has no training?" Julia insisted.

"No," Martin said. "I've taken her to doctors and religious leaders, but they couldn't help us." He glanced at Heather and gave her a small smile. "Your granddaughter has taken pity on me and shown us kindness."

"It's not pity." Heather rubbed his arm lightly.

"You're a good father. You just didn't know what you were dealing with. Now you do."

"I knew you'd find your next chapter," Julia said, smiling. She glanced at Vivien. "Aren't they cute together? Such a handsome couple."

"They really are," Vivien agreed with a tiny laugh.

"Oh, we're not," Martin tried to correct. "I mean, I'd want to if things were different, but I have to take care of Jan, and she's my boss, and—"

"If you're not attracted to her, just tell her. She's a big girl. She can take it," Julia said.

"But I am attracted to..." His words trailed off into a groan. He clearly did not mean to reveal as much.

Pleasure erupted inside Heather at the slip.

"Don't worry, champ," Vivien quipped, slapping him on the shoulder. "Better men have gone up against Julia's cunning and failed." To Heather, she added, "Told you that you'd be dating the sexy construction guy. It's such a pain being right all the time."

Julia chuckled. "They never listen, do they?"

Vivien shook her head in denial. "Never. You think they'd learn to trust everything I say as truth."

"So what can I do for you, Martin?" Julia asked.

"You're doing it. He needed to see a real ghost to understand what his daughter is going through." Heather threaded her fingers in front of her and looked down.

"What else?" Julia prompted.

"We tried to see what's haunting Old Anderson House so we held a séance," Heather said.

"That's a silly waste. Nothing is haunting Old Anderson House," Julia answered. "What did I tell you? Just because a building is old doesn't mean spirits have moved in. It might increase the odds, but it's hardly an indicator."

"I didn't think so either. And you're right. It wasn't. Jan was. She was hiding in there, and when we tried to summon the spirit we thought might be in the house, about a dozen appeared. They were all tied to her. I think we got a handful of them to move on, but I'm pretty sure some stayed."

"Not all spirits are meant to move on," Julia said. "Some of us belong here because we choose it. Some are trapped because of something that happened in life."

Julia reached a hand toward Heather's cheek, but all she felt was the sensation of cold.

"Can you look for us and make sure none of the

spirits hanging out by her are dangerous?" Heather asked.

"I can try," Julia agreed.

"Can you tell them they need to stop telling her to do bad things?" Martin added. "Tell them to leave her alone. And to stay away from her. She needs privacy."

"They won't leave her alone completely, not if she's acknowledged them already. It's lonely on this side sometimes. It's difficult to be part of the world but not seen or heard, and many can only affect it in small degrees." Julia moved to study his face. "My granddaughter is right. You're a good man and a good father. I see that in your aura. You just keep loving her the best you know how. Heather and I will make sure she knows she's not alone."

Martin nodded. "Thank you. All of you. This is the closest I've come to understanding what Jan must be going through since she was born."

"Of course." Julia's smile was soft. "Heather did right in bringing this to my attention."

"Lorna, you're quiet." Julia moved toward her, walking instead of flashing around from place to place. "How have you been, love?"

"Good, thank you," Lorna said.

"No more nightmares?" Julia inquired. "No more thinking about Glenn?"

Lorna smiled. "No."

"Who's Glenn?" Martin asked.

"An asshole," Vivien stated.

"Her late husband," Heather said, more diplomatically.

"Who was an asshole," Vivien insisted.

"At the funeral I learned he had another wife. He lied to me for twenty years," Lorna explained, simplifying her situation. "It's a long story. I'm sure if the other wife has her way, you'll be able to read all about her plight someday."

"I'm sorry." Martin frowned. "That sounds horrible."

"Thank you. It was." Lorna ran her fingers through her hair and turned her face away.

Julia's body faded. "I'm a little tired, girls."

"Wait, Grandma." Heather hurried forward and quietly asked, "Have you seen Trav around at all since we talked last?"

Julia shook her head and tried to speak, but the sound didn't come out of her moving lips. The overhead lights flickered. Julia disappeared.

"What happened?" Martin looked around. "Where did she go?"

"That's it," Vivien said. "She's gone for now."

Martin moved to take the seat Lorna had offered him earlier. He leaned forward and grabbed his head in his hands. His elbows braced against his knees. "I don't feel so well."

"You need sugar." Lorna went to grab the cake.

"It will help," Vivien added.

Heather went to kneel beside him. "The light-headedness is normal. Spirits borrow a lot of energy to manifest. It's why the lights flicker, and it's why you feel the way you do now."

"It's not that." Martin kept his head down. "All these years."

"What about them?" Heather tried to lean over to make him look at her, but his eyes were closed.

"All these years I didn't believe her. My daughter tried to tell me what was going on with her, and I thought she had a mental illness. I took her to all those doctors. They put her through all those tests." His eyes were tortured when he looked up. "She was telling me she was in pain and alone, and I didn't believe her."

"How could you know?" Lorna asked, pulling out the cake pan and paper plate. "You can't beat yourself up for that."

"Shh," Vivien insisted suddenly. She lifted her hands. "Something's not right."

Heather stood. "What?"

Vivien stiffened. "Something's going on with William and Jan. We have to go."

"Jan?" Martin surged to his feet and hurried toward the edge of the stage. "What is it? Is she hurt? Where are they?"

CHAPTER TWELVE

"HEATHER!" William's shout came from the front of the lobby as Martin ran down the aisle toward it. "Heather, I need you!"

"Where is she? What happened?" Martin demanded as he burst into the lobby. He looked around before running to the front doors to look outside at the darkened street. "Jan!"

"She's not here," William said, fighting for the words as he gulped for air. Sweat poured down the sides of his face and stained his shirt.

"Where is she?" Martin made a move as if to grab William by the shirt. She knew that panic coursing through him well. It raged inside of her just like it had all those years ago when her son couldn't be found. There was no fear like it.

"Martin, stop," Heather cried as her brother dodged the man. "That's not helping."

"Where is my daughter?" Martin demanded.

"No one told me she knew how to hotwire my truck," William defended. "Or drive."

"What?" Martin went back to the glass doors to look out. "She doesn't drive."

"Jan stole my truck and took off. We were having pizza. Things were fine, or whatever, and then she said she had to use the restroom. It's not like I was going to follow her in there to make sure she went. The waitress came and got me because she saw Jan driving off in my truck." He reached into his pocket to pull out his keys to show them he still had them. "I tried calling all of you, but no one picked up."

"Julia must have drained our phones," Lorna said. "It worked. Martin saw her."

"I figured that might be the case so I ran here," William said. "Does anyone have any idea where Jan would go?"

"Did you report the truck stolen to the police?" Lorna asked.

"I wasn't sure what to do," William admitted. "I don't want to get her in trouble if she's with a ghost, but then it's not safe for a ten-year-old to be behind the wheel. It sounded like the girl has enough troubles. I didn't want to put legal ones on her too. It's only been like ten minutes. I ran straight here. I have my phone. Do you want me to report it?"

"I think I know where she might go," Martin said.

"Anderson House," Heather and Vivien said in unison.

"She's obsessed with that place." Martin pushed through the doors, and they followed him out.

"Man, I'm sorry. I had no idea she'd run off," William called after him.

"I should have mentioned she might do that. She acts out sometimes," Martin answered. "I'm going to check the house."

"William, lock up. My keys are in my purse." Heather followed Martin. "Meet us over there."

"Go," William yelled.

Heather ran to the passenger side door and climbed into Martin's truck without asking. She felt dizzy from the séance, and without sugar the sensation would only get worse. But that hardly mattered right now. "I'm sure she's fine."

"This is the worst part." Martin tapped his fingers on the steering wheel in agitation as he drove. "The not knowing where she is when she runs off like this, whether she's safe or hurt."

Heather remembered the feeling well. Her hands

began to shake. Tears fought their way to her eyes. Maybe they should call the police—the more people looking the better.

"I can't believe she took off," Martin continued. "What was she thinking?"

"I don't know," Heather said. She found herself searching the streets for signs of William's truck. "But I don't think the ghosts want to hurt her."

The thought wouldn't be that comforting to a parent.

"One night. That's all I needed. One night to try and understand what she's going through, and then she pulls this stunt." Martin hit his hand against the wheel in frustration. "Dammit! I thought it would be easier knowing what was going on with her, but how in the hell do I fight ghosts? If she was hanging out with the wrong crowd at school, I could get her away from that. I could set up security alarms and ground her to her room to think about her actions. But ghosts? They bypass alarms. My daughter can bypass alarms, thanks to them. I know. I tried that too."

Heather knew he was panicked and ranting in worry, so she let him talk. There was no right way to handle a situation like this. Martin had been through a lot in a short time. Finding proof of the supernatural would be hard for anyone to process.

Heck, she'd known ghosts were real her entire life, and, recently, even she'd been apprehensive at the idea that she might not be able to see all of them. For a regular guy, Martin was handling it better than most.

The truck took a corner a little too fast, and Heather slid on the seat closer to him.

"I don't know what to do," Martin whispered, frustration seeping from him.

"Yes, you do," Heather said calmly, touching his arm in an attempt to comfort him a little. "You're a good father, Martin. You're going to find her like you always do. Then you're going to tell her what happened tonight, and that you believe her, and that you're sorry you didn't before. You're going to tell her that you love her no matter what."

Martin nodded. He sped toward Anderson House.

"You're not alone in this anymore. Viv, Lorna, and I will help you," Heather continued. She tried to push past the knot in her chest as images tried to surface of the night she'd lost her son. It was impossible not to feel that same fear as Martin searched for his daughter.

They neared the house. Martin pulled the truck along the curb, stuck it in park, and jumped out while the engine was still running. He ran toward the front door. "Jan!"

He tried to pull it open, but the door was locked.

Heather looked up toward the third story. The house was dark.

Martin came back down the steps only to run around the side of the house. "January, answer me!"

Heather followed him to the back door. He pulled at the handle, but it was locked as well. "I don't see my brother's truck. Where else would she go?"

"I don't..." Martin frowned. He pulled his phone out of his pocket. "I don't know. Home maybe? I think I need to call the police."

Heather didn't stop him. The more people out looking, the better.

His hand shook as he dialed. "What if there was an accident? What was she thinking?"

The glow of headlights caught their attention, followed by the sound of a revved motor. Martin stopped mid-dial and ran toward the front of the house. "January!"

William pulled along the curb in her car and rolled down the driver's side window. "Heather, we need to go. Mom called. No one could get ahold of you, so they called her, and she called me."

"Did they find her?" Martin asked. "What happened?"

William shook his head.

"Who called her?" Heather asked.

"The fire department. They're at your house. It's on fire. A neighbor called it in." He didn't get out of the car. "Lorna and Vivien are on their way there. I told mom to let them know you're not in the house so no one tries to go in looking for you."

"But..." Heather glanced between William and Martin as she processed what he was saying.

"You go," Martin said. "I need to find my daughter."

"It's just a house. I'll deal with it later," Heather said, unable to fully process what was happening. Stress manifested as a tear and rolled down her cheek. She thought of her son, of Jan, of the fear that choked her and made her want to vomit. "We need to find Jan."

"I'm going to check my house," Martin said. "Hopefully she went home."

She thought of the picture Jan had drawn of Heather crying as Old Anderson House went up in flames.

"Omigod," Heather whispered before shouting,

"The house. Jan!" She ran toward the truck. "I think she might be at my house."

"Why would she go there?" Martin asked.

"Just trust me," Heather said. She waved at her brother. "Go, go! Tell Viv."

William took off as they jumped in Martin's truck.

Heather motioned after William. "Follow him."

Martin threw the truck into gear and sped after William.

"Did you get a message from a ghost?" Martin asked. "Is Jan all right?"

"I think Jan left me the message," Heather answered. With all of the emotions flooding her, it was difficult to explain. "We found this drawing she did of me standing in front of a fire."

"What? When?" Martin demanded. "Why didn't you tell me?"

"The other day at Anderson House," Heather said. "I wasn't sure what to make of it. Then you caught us holding a séance, and Jan was upset because we sent her friends away, and I guess I forgot about it. A creepy picture didn't seem all that important."

Martin gripped the wheel as he followed William down her street. Heather leaned forward in her seat and looked up. An orange glow in the sky from the fire acted like a beacon in the night. The flash of emergency responder lights bounced off the trees as they rounded a curve.

Heather's heart nearly dropped. Flames engulfed the back of her house. Neighbors had begun to gather across the street.

She was so stunned, focusing on her burning house, that she almost missed William's truck along the side of the road, parked halfway onto the sidewalk. She pointed at it. "William's truck. Jan's here."

Martin was forced to pull over as the emergency vehicles blocked the road. He shut off the engine, and they jumped out of his truck. Heather ran to William's truck and looked inside. Jan was not inside.

"She's not here," she said, before yelling, "Jan! Can you hear me?"

Even as Heather said the words, she began moving toward her house. She searched the crowd for the child as she half walked, half jogged toward the fire trucks. Some of her neighbors tried to get her attention, but she couldn't hear their words over the sound of her heart pounding in her ears.

"Do you see her?" Martin asked.

Heather shook her head. Seeing her brother near

a fire truck talking to a police officer, she hurried over to him.

"—a girl inside the house," William was saying. "She's about ten. We can't find her."

"What happened?" Heather asked, recognizing the officer. Bacuzzi had been a few years ahead of her in school. No one had been surprised when he joined the police force. It would have either been that or a military career.

"We're not sure," Officer Bacuzzi answered. He held up his finger and grabbed the radio on his shoulder. As he rushed away from them, he said, "Be advised, we have possible reports of a ten-year-old girl inside the house."

Almost instantly shouts sounded as the firefighters received the news.

"Did you see my truck?" William asked. "She's here."

"Heather," Vivien's voice called. She and Lorna came from the crowd. "Did you find her?"

Heather shook her head. Martin pushed past them, trying to get closer to the fire as he looked frantically around.

"The drawing," Heather said.

"We thought of that too." Lorna crossed her arms over her chest, hugging herself in concern.

A tear rolled down Heather's cheek. "You don't think she's in there, do you?"

Heather hated to lose her house, but it was just a house. That wasn't what was important.

"No," Vivien said, though she didn't sound confident in the answer.

"There has to be something we can do." Lorna dropped her arms. "What is the point of having magic if we can't use it right now?"

Heather looked at the crowd.

"She's right," William said. "You have to try it. Who cares if the whole town sees you?"

Coming from William, who had always shied away from talking about the family secret, that was a huge statement. Heather knew he felt guilty over losing Jan while he was responsible for her.

"Over there." Vivien pointed to a shadowed area down the street where they could hide behind a few bushes.

"William, find Martin," Lorna said.

The three women ran until they were under a tree, hidden mostly from view. They joined hands, feeling the magic surge between them. Their hair lifted from their shoulders.

"If anyone is here with us, show yourself," Vivien ordered.

"We're looking for a little girl," Heather added, talking to what looked to be empty space. "Please, if anyone is here, we need your help. The girl's name is Jan. She's special, like us. Maybe you've talked to her? Maybe you've seen her? We need your help."

"Left, left," a fireman shouted.

"Oh, now you want to talk."

Heather stiffened. "Did you hear that?"

"No," Vivien and Lorna said in unison.

"Who's there?" Heather demanded.

The erratic ghost who'd followed her into Anderson House appeared. The last time Heather saw her, she'd told the woman to buzz off. The spirit had not been too pleased with her.

"Like, why should I help you? You totally couldn't be bothered to talk to me when I tried to tell you that my husband shoved me overboard so he could be with his mistress. She's grody to the max." The ghost placed her hands on her hips. *"I bet you don't even remember my name."*

"You never gave it to me," Heather said. "What's your name?"

"Who is it?" Lorna asked.

"Can they help?" Vivien insisted.

Her friends couldn't see the spirit without a proper séance.

Heather didn't answer them. The ghost was difficult to hear on a good day, and with the roar of the fire and the shouts of the firefighters, it became nearly impossible. She let go of her friend's hands and angled her ear toward the ghost.

"Muffy," the spirit answered.

"Muffy, help me now, and I promise I will help you in any way that I can," Heather stated. The fact the one spirit that had answered the call for help looked and sounded like a California party girl from the 1980s was not comforting in the least. But they didn't have a choice. Beggars could not be choosers.

"Can't and won't. That is what you said to me. I both can't and won't."

"Did you do this?" Heather demanded. So help Muffy, if she was behind the fire and the threat to Jan's life, Heather would stop at nothing to exorcise her ass into the darkest regions of the afterlife. It couldn't be a coincidence that this was the spirit who showed up as soon as they called out to the other side. "Did you lead Jan here and start this fire to get back at me?"

"Can't and won't," Muffy repeated, hands on hips.

"Answer me now," Heather ordered. "Did you do this?"

"I only made a few phone calls. This disaster is not my fault."

That is why her phone had been ringing all night? Somehow, that explanation fit what little she'd seen of Muffy's personality.

"Can't and won't," Muffy grumbled, tossing her head back and forth to enunciate her anger.

"But you can. I need you to look into the house and tell me if a little girl is trapped anywhere. Please, she needs your help. Do not punish her because you're angry at me."

"Do you think that I would hurt a little girl to get even with you? You think very highly of yourself. Maybe you should, like, look into that."

"I will," Heather said.

The ghost huffed and then disappeared.

"Well?" Vivien asked.

"We need to find someone else." Heather held out her hands so they could retry. "I have a feeling Muffy the ghost will probably stop off at the mall first."

More shouts came from the firefighters.

"She's not there." Muffy reappeared.

Heather gave a small jolt of surprise, pulling her hands away to turn back around. Muffy stood with her hands on her hips and a superior look on her features.

"What?" Lorna prompted.

"Muffy said she's not—"

A burst of flames lit the sky as something exploded. Heather cried out in fear.

"Jan!" Martin's shout came from beyond the trucks.

"Stop that man," someone ordered.

"Are you sure?" Heather demanded, facing Muffy. She wished she could grab onto the ghost and shake the answers out of her. Tears rolled down Heather's face. "You have to tell me. Did you look everywhere? Her name is January. She's this tall." Heather held out her hand.

"Please help us," Vivien added even though she couldn't see or hear the ghost.

"She has dark hair and is a little shy," Heather continued. "Right now she's probably feeling very alone. We have to find her. We—"

"*Ugh, you talk so much.*" Muffy held up her hands. "*I don't, like, know if it's her or whatever, but a girl is hiding out, crying.*"

"Where?"

Muffy pointed toward a neighbor's yard.

"She's over there," Heather said. "Find Martin and William and let them know."

Vivien and Lorna ran to look for Martin. Heather pushed through a row of shrubbery to cross into her neighbor's backyard. In the evenings, their boxer was tied up by the doghouse, but she didn't see the dog running the yard like he usually did.

"Jan, are you out here? January, it's me, Heather." Heather searched the bushes. "Sweetheart, if you're here, I need you to answer me."

A thump came from within the doghouse. Heather instantly went to investigate. She leaned over, trying to see inside. The boxer laid on what looked to be a lap. It was hard to make out details in the darkness.

"Jan? We've been looking everywhere for you." Heather kept her voice soft.

The leg shifted, and the dog lifted its head.

"Jan, honey, I need you to come out. Everyone is so worried about you. Your dad's looking for you right now. He's so scared." Heather soothed.

The boxer roused and came out of the doghouse. He wagged his tail as he came toward Heather for attention. She petted him to keep him from jumping on her.

"I can't," Jan answered, the word sounding

strained as if she held back tears. "Dad's going to be so mad at me. I didn't want to do it. I didn't want to. He made me promise."

"Who? Who made you promise?" Heather inched closer. "Your dad? If he's mad, I'm sure it's just because he cares for you so much and was worried when you ran off. He loves you so much."

Jan poked her head out of the doghouse and looked at her. Tears streaked her cheeks. Her eyes and nose were red.

"Not my dad." Jan crawled out. She cradled her hand against her stomach. A bit of blood stained her t-shirt.

"Did you hurt yourself?" Heather reached for her. "Let me see."

Jan held out her hand to show where she'd cut herself. It appeared deep.

"How did this happen?" Heather lightly pushed the boxer away as he playfully tried to jump between them.

Jan shrugged and moved to pet the dog.

"Did you have something to do with the fire?" Heather asked.

Jan kept her attention on the animal. Tears filled her eyes, and she moaned softly.

Heather gently took her arm and pulled her from

the dog's reach. The boxer bounced around, softly whining as he wanted them to play. The dog lived in a family with three children and had plenty of playmates during the day.

"I need you to tell me the truth," Heather said. "I promise I won't be angry if you tell me what happened tonight. But we do need to talk about this. Stealing trucks and setting fires is not okay. Someone could've gotten seriously hurt, or worse. You could have been killed."

"It was him." The girl lifted her hand and pointed behind Heather. "He made me promise to help him."

Heather turned to look. She caught a glimpse of a figure before Martin, Vivien, Lorna, and William came through the hedge. The ghostly figure disappeared but not before she saw her son's face.

Heather pushed her feet in desperation. She ran to where the ghost had been. "Trav?"

His name barely made it past her lips as it stuck in her throat. Her heart pounded, and she couldn't breathe. She shook violently, caught between hope and agony.

Her son.

Travis.

Her sweet boy.

This time she was positive she had seen him. She recognized the striped shirt he'd been wearing the day he died and the torn jeans. The rip had been from falling off his skateboard. Man how they had fought over that. She'd been so angry because they were school clothes. It all seems so stupid now.

"Jan..." Martin's word trailed off as he ran to his daughter. Heather didn't turn around to look, but she didn't need to. She knew the relief he had to be feeling. It was the relief she had dreamed about but had never gotten for herself. When they found her son, the ending had been a much different story.

"Heather, what is it?" Vivien came to where Heather stood near the bushes blocking the way back to her house.

"You found her," William said, sounding relieved.

"Do you feel that?" Lorna lifted her hand toward Heather as she spoke to Vivien.

Heather knew they were detecting the pain that radiated off her. She didn't care. She couldn't hide it or bury it deep inside. She had seen her son's face. He had been here.

And he disappeared when she saw him.

He didn't want to see her.

Was he angry at her?

Had he been around the entire time?

Did he blame her for not taking care of him, as she had spent the last decade blaming herself?

She was his mother. She had one job. It was her responsibility to keep him safe. She had failed. How could she fault him if he blamed her?

"Trav?" she whispered. The salt of her tears filled her mouth as they wet her lips.

Heather sobbed, crying out in pain. Vivien grabbed hold of her shoulders when she would fall to the ground.

"Did you see him?" Vivien asked.

"Is Travis here?" William looked around as if he could find his nephew, even though they all knew he wouldn't.

Heather nodded, unable to speak.

Lorna pulled her into a hug, helping to keep her upright. Her hands stroked Heather's back.

"What is it?" Martin asked. He held Jan in his arms as she held on tight to his neck.

"Her son," Vivien answered.

"She saw her son," Lorna said at the same time.

"Come back, my sweet boy," Heather insisted, willing him to appear.

"I'm sorry, Daddy," Jan cried. "He made me

promise to help him. Don't be mad at me. I had to help my friend."

"Shh, baby," Martin soothed. "It's going to be okay. I've got you."

When Heather met his eyes briefly, she saw his fear. It was obvious that his daughter had something to do with the fire. However a the-ghost-made-me-do-it defense would not play out well in court.

Then again, maybe her son was also to blame for the fire.

Now that Jan was safe, Heather looked in the direction of her house. The flames were slowly coming under control. It appeared like most of the damage was focused on the back of the house near her son's bedroom.

She had just looked inside the room. Everything had been the way he'd left it. The toys he had touched, the bed he'd forgotten to make, the shoes shoved in the corner, all of it was in there. And now it was gone. She could care less about her tax documents and high school yearbooks, or any number of material items. But her son's room?

Heather couldn't hold the tears at bay any longer. So many emotions whirled within her that it became impossible to keep them buried. She was still so angry that Trav had been taken from her. It wasn't fair. None of this was fair. What had she done to deserve this?

Her life had stopped that day. It ended a happy marriage. It cut short a beautiful life.

All the lists in the world were not bringing her back from this moment. For a decade she'd been hanging on by a thread. Somehow having that room the way he'd left it kept her close to him. Like some deep illogical part of her believed he might come back. Someday. Somehow. Even as a ghost, he would be her son. His room would be waiting for him. She would be waiting for him. For all eternity.

These thoughts had never fully formed before now. Heather had not been aware of what she'd been doing, not completely. But now that it was gone, she felt the loss as greatly as the moment it had happened.

"It's not your fault," Lorna whispered. Both she and Vivien touched Heather, feeling the emotions raging inside her. There was no hiding from her friends. They could read all her secrets even if she didn't want them to.

"It's just a room, Heather. It's just a house," Vivien said. "No one can take your memories from you."

"He doesn't want to see me," Heather answered.

"He's here and he can show himself, but he doesn't want to see *me*. He went to her."

Heather looked at Jan, ashamed of the jealousy she felt. She knew Jan was just a child, and it wasn't her fault. But it hurt. Badly. Her son had gone to Jan, not her. In the afterlife, he had to know that Heather had gifts and that she had been looking for him. She'd called out to him so many times.

"I can't believe that's true," William countered. "Your son loves you. You were a terrific mother."

Lorna and Vivien continued to hold onto her. Heather was thankful for their support. Without it she would've fallen to the ground in a heap of emotion and not gotten back up.

Jan's shoulders shook as her father continue to hold her. Her lips moved, but Heather couldn't hear what she was saying. Martin nodded and patted the girl's back. Heather looked at him expectantly.

Martin had a hard time meeting her gaze. He looked at the ground. "She says that..."

"What?" Vivien prompted when it became clear Martin would not finish the sentence.

"She says that the fire wasn't her idea," Martin answered with a deep breath. He glanced at Heather and then back down at her feet. "It was your son's. He begged her to set the fire for him because he couldn't. He said he tried. He doesn't want you living in that house anymore. He doesn't want you looking at his room and crying."

"He doesn't want to see you so sad," Jan's tiny voice added. "He made me promise not to let you go back there. He said…"

"What?" Heather pushed out of her friend's hold and stepped closer to Martin and Jan. "What did he say? Tell me. Please."

"He said his dad had a new baby to take care of," Jan answered. "He wants you to have someone to take care of too."

"Ben has another child?" Heather looked at William. "I hadn't heard."

William shook his head, indicating he knew nothing about it.

"I bet that's why mom tried to get me to send pictures to Ben out of the blue the other day. She probably heard the news and wanted me to talk to him so I could find out for myself." Heather ran her hands through her hair. Staticky strands stuck to her skin from the use of magic. "She should have just told me."

A light vibrating sound came from William's pocket. He pulled out his phone.

"Mom," William said.

"Take care of it?" Heather begged. "I can't right now."

William nodded but didn't answer the phone right away. "We should let the police know we found Jan and that she's safe. I'll go tell them." He held up the ringing phone. "And I would be surprised if mom isn't by the firetrucks freaking out because she can't find us. I'll take care of it."

William answered the call. "Hey, Mom, are you here? Where are you? I don't see you."

"We will need to say something to the fire department about how this happened," Vivien said. She looked at Martin.

"I..." Martin had set Jan on her feet but kept his arm around her shoulders. It was apparent none of them were sure what to do.

"We can't tell them what happened," Heather said.

"They know we're looking for Jan," Lorna said.

"We lie our asses off," Vivien stated. "We'll tell them William was mistaken. Jan was supposed to be at your house tonight, Heather, but you had to run an errand for work, so you dropped her off with me instead. In the confusion, William thought Jan was still in your house because she got scared by the fire and hid, and we couldn't find her."

"No one will be surprised that Heather is upset and a little frazzled. I mean, it is her house," Lorna reasoned.

Heather rubbed her face. Her swollen sinuses and burning eyes made it unmistakable that she had been crying.

"What if they investigate and realize it's arson?" Martin asked. "They might think you had something to do with it, Heather."

"Jan, how did you start the fire? Matches? Did you use gasoline or anything to make it bigger?" Vivien asked, trying to determine what the investigators might find when this was over.

Jan shook her head. "He told me to plug in the heater in his room, put a blanket over it, and open the window. The blanket caught fire and then made the wall spark."

Martin closed his eyes. "I can't believe I'm hearing this."

"Okay, I say the plan is to lie our asses off and hope they think it's an electrical fire," Vivien decided for the group. "If we all stick to our stories, then they'll have to believe us."

Heather was glad somebody was thinking clearly because her thoughts were all over the place.

"Heather has no criminal history. She's not in

financial trouble. There's no motive for her to set her own house on fire," Lorna added. "She is a valued member of this community. She does so much for the people here. I'm sure many would stand up in protest if they tried to pin this on her."

"This might not be the best plan we've ever come up with, but it's the only plan we have right now," Vivien said. "Try to say as little as possible tonight. In all the chaos, I'm sure we can get out of making statements until later, but if we are asked questions, then we know what to say. Jan, honey, if anybody asks you a question just start crying and refuse to answer. Don't say anything to anyone about this. Do you understand?"

Jan nodded.

"I'm going to need you to say the words. Say that you understand," Vivien insisted. "This is very important."

"Yes," Jan whispered. "I understand."

"Good girl." Vivien nodded at her in approval.

"This feels wrong on so many levels," Martin said. "But I don't have a better idea of what to do. Thank you for trying to protect my daughter. I..." He sighed. "Just thank you."

"Heather, you should be seen." Lorna motioned that they should go back toward the firetrucks. "We'll stay with you. Then when this is over, you'll come home with Viv and me. You should not be alone tonight." Lorna looked at Martin. "Actually, I don't think any of us should be alone tonight. You should bring Jan over to our house as well. That way, we can all keep an eye on her. If she tries to leave, the motion sensors will go off and alert Vivien's phone."

"Yes. That's a good idea." Heather nodded. It would be safer for all of them to stay together, but Heather had other reasons as well. If her son came back to talk to Jan, she wanted to be there. She needed to see him. She needed to know that he was all right. She needed him to know that she loved him.

Jan's hand caught her attention.

"Jan, show Lorna your cut," Heather said.

"What cut?" Martin looked down in surprise as Jan lifted her hand.

"That looks deep," Lorna said. "Does it hurt?"

Jan gave a slight nod.

"What happened?" Martin asked.

Jan shrugged.

Heather held out her hand to Lorna. "Transfer it."

"What it?" Martin frowned.

"Want to see a magic trick?" Lorna asked.

Jan stared at her, eyes wide and unsure.

"This might tickle," Lorna said, taking Jan's hand in her own. Heather could tell that Lorna was planning on keeping the injury for herself.

Heather grabbed Lorna's free hand. "No tricks. You're giving it to me."

Lorna frowned but didn't argue. From the outside looking in, it appeared as if nothing happened. There was no great magical show of lights. It looked like the three of them were just holding hands. Heather felt the tingling where they touched. Jan made a slight noise of surprise. The injury flowed from Jan's hand through Lorna to become embedded in Heather's palm. Instantly the wound stung and throbbed.

When Lorna finished and released them, Heather stretched her fingers to test the injury.

"Dad, look." Jan held up her uninjured hand to show him.

"What...? How?" Martin took Heather's hand in his to look at it.

"Lorna is a healer," Heather said. "You have enough to deal with right now."

"And you don't?" he countered.

"I can take care of a cut better than she can." Heather watched him trace along the edge of the wound. "I'll clean it out and superglue it shut later."

MICHELLE M. PILLOW

"You really are something special," Martin murmured in amazement. "After everything she's put you through, you're still trying to help her."

"From the sounds of things, both of our kids are to blame for what's happening," Heather said.

"Can you teach me how to do that?" Jan asked Lorna.

"I'm not sure I can," Lorna answered. "I think maybe we need to talk about controlling what you can already do before we start trying to add new things."

"Then it's decided," Vivien stated. "Slumber party at my house tonight. And Heather, you're living with us until you decide what you're going to do. Don't bother protesting. There is no way in hell we're letting you be alone right now."

CHAPTER THIRTEEN

THE SMELL of charred wood and wet ash overpowered every other scent. There appeared to be a distinct line of demarcation between the front and the back, from the front door that looked untouched to the charcoaled remains of the back. It was as if a fiery dragon had taken a bite out of it. Inside the damage might not be as clearly defined, but she wouldn't be able to look until the fire department cleared the site.

In the light from the firetrucks, she saw the sheen of dripping water against piles of rubble. That had been her office, and her bathroom, and her son's room. Oddly, the toilet had survived, but the roof had caved in on the sink and shower. She found herself staring at the porcelain throne amidst the ruin. There was a joke in there somewhere, but she was too tired to think of it.

"The utilities are turned off," Officer Bacuzzi informed her. "Do you have any valuables in the home that need to be secured?"

My son's room, but that's gone now.

"The fire safe in the office." She pointed to where the office had been. "And the antique jewelry box on my bedroom dresser. There's also some cash in the nightstand."

"I'll have the guys secure those for you before they leave," Bacuzzi said. "Give me a second. I'll be right back."

"Shit." Heather grimaced as she thought of her nightstand.

"What?" Vivien asked. "You're doing great."

"My silicone boyfriend is in the nightstand," Heather muttered so only her friends could hear.

Lorna nearly choked on her bottle of water.

"I shouldn't have told him about the cash I keep in there. I'm never going to hear the end of this." Heather put her hands on her head. "Dammit."

"I'll take care of it." Vivien moved to follow Bacuzzi. "Bac, wait up!"

William appeared next to Lorna, pausing to kiss

her cheek. He held out an array of candy bars. "Eat these."

Heather grabbed one, not bothering to look at what kind she chose. After a séance and the emotional aftermath, she desperately needed the sugar.

"Where's mom?" Heather asked.

"I told her you hadn't eaten all day and suggested she make some casseroles for you tomorrow to help out. She needed a task," William said. "Troy went with her to get the groceries. He'll drop mom off at home and then bring take out over to Vivien's for us. I didn't think you wanted her hanging around asking questions and trying to hold you while you're making a statement to the cops."

Bonnie had hugged her for nearly five minutes, talking about how scared she was when the fire department called her and said they couldn't get ahold of her baby girl.

"You're a really good brother." Heather bit into the candy.

Lorna took a couple of candy bars from William and held them out as Martin and Jan approached. "Eat these."

Martin took them from her. "Jan?"

Jan took a candy bar and went to sit on the curb.

"All good?" Heather asked.

Martin nodded. "They didn't ask much. Just verified that Jan was safe."

"You should eat that chocolate. You have to be drained." Heather took another bite.

"The sugar helps after we..." Lorna glanced to see if Jan could hear them. "After we talk to Julia."

Vivien returned. "I took care of it."

Heather took her at her word. "Thank you."

"Candy?" William held out his stash.

"Yes, please." Vivien grabbed one and tore it open.

Heather looked at the tired line of her friends and began to laugh.

"What's so funny?" William asked.

"I don't know." Heather shrugged. "Just us. Eating candy, here, now."

"Okay, I think it's time we got you home," Vivien said.

Bacuzzi returned, carrying her jewelry box. "The guys are bringing out your safe. Do you have some place you'd like to store it?"

"I'll pull my truck around," William said. He took the jewelry box from the officer and then left to fetch his vehicle.

"I'll make sure patrol cars keep an eye on the

house until you can get a crew out here to board up the back. The fire department will send someone out to look at the damage first thing in the morning. They'll call you with the all clear. Depending on what they find, a detective could contact you for a follow-up. In the meantime, get ahold of your insurance." He pulled a card from his uniform pocket. "Give them my email. I'll have a report number assigned tomorrow so you can get the ball rolling. And make sure you keep receipts for anything you spend regarding this or items that you have to replace. Trust me. You'll want those for your insurance and your tax accountant. My cousin learned that lesson the hard way."

"Thank you." Heather took his card. "I appreciate all you've done tonight."

"I'm just glad no one was hurt," Bacuzzi answered. "I have everything I need. You're free to go."

Heather looked at Jan. The girl held a candy bar, but it didn't look like she'd eaten much.

"You heard the man," Vivien said. "There's nothing else we can do tonight. Let's get out of here."

CHAPTER FOURTEEN

"I think I can sleep for a century." Heather fell more than sat on the couch next to Martin. She had borrowed Vivien's pajama pants and t-shirt. Her hair was damp from her shower and had wet the back of her shirt. She was too tired to care. "Jan has had a bath and is asleep on Vivien's bedroom floor. Lorna made her a fort out of blankets and chairs. I'm not sure who liked it more. Viv fell asleep in there with her."

Lorna was with William in her bedroom. Vivien had made up a bed for Martin on the couch. The only person missing was Troy, but after he'd brought them all burgers and fries, he went to his own home next door.

"Are you sure this isn't a bother?" Martin asked.

He had used Lorna's bathroom to clean up. His hair had started to dry. Vivien had borrowed sweatpants and a shirt from Troy for him to use. The t-shirt fitted a little snug across the shoulders.

"You know that saying, takes a village? Well, like it or not, we're your village," Heather said.

"I like it." Martin's tone dropped, and he smiled. He leaned back next to her on the couch and turned to face her. Their heads rested against the back cushions. "After everything that happened tonight, I can't believe you're still so..."

"So?"

"So calm. So nice. So forgiving. So understanding." His hand lifted to touch her face. "So beautiful."

A tiny shiver of awareness ran down her neck at his touch. When she didn't stop him, he brought his hand more fully against her cheek.

"Would it be out of line if I kissed you right now?" he asked.

Heather couldn't speak. She shook her head.

"Good, because I've been thinking about kissing you for months, since that first time we met," he admitted. "You needed those light fixtures hung."

"You never showed it," Heather said.

His thumb touched her bottom lip in a soft

caress. "Good to know I can play it cool because I was sure you noticed that I couldn't take my eyes off of you. I wanted to ask you out, but, you know, I have Jan."

"I like Jan," Heather said.

"You're an amazing woman, Heather. I've never known anyone like you." His hand against her face mesmerized her senses.

As she gazed into his eyes, the world felt small and safe. Her magic tingled down her hand from Julia's ring, trying to connect her to him. Deep attraction unfurled between them.

What was he waiting for?

"You should kiss me now," she whispered.

Martin leaned toward her. His fingers slid into her wet hair. The first brush of his lips awakened a part of her that had laid dormant for far too long. Her heart quickened as she anticipated a deeper caress.

Heather hadn't been intimate with a man for a long time, but it wasn't like her ex-husband had been her one and only. She touched his chest, letting her hand explore the muscles beneath the cotton t-shirt. The material pulled tight against well-built biceps. There was no denying he was a handsome man.

Martin's tongue moved along the seam of her lips, urging them to part. She allowed him to deepen the kiss. Each tiny movement seemed to be a test. His hand moved from her jaw down her throat. When she pushed her tongue to meet his, the hand moved to her collarbone.

What am I doing?

Heather knew there was some logical thought she should be having, but his lips felt so right. Her skin ached to be touched. She wanted to explore the pleasure he offered.

She removed her hand from his chest and grabbed his forearm, pressing down so that his hand ventured lower to a breast. Martin moaned as his palm fit against the soft globe. Her nipple tightened.

Heather broke their kiss as she adjusted on the couch. She touched his waist, lifting the material so she could feel the texture of his skin. Her fingers dipped along his waistband.

"Should we be doing this here?" Martin whispered. He kneaded her breast with firm strokes.

"Everyone's asleep." Heather pushed her hand deeper to touch his naked hip, so there was no mistaking what she asked for.

Martin released her breast long enough to push his hand beneath the cami she wore under the t-shirt. Heather bit her lip to keep from moaning too loudly. His hands were rough from construction work and felt wonderful against her skin. She pushed her hand deeper, feeling his ass against her palm.

Heather leaned back, and he followed her as she lay down. The new position allowed his body to settle against her. The unmistakable shape of his arousal pressed against her hip.

"I think I know where Viv keeps her condoms," she said.

"I have one in my wallet," he answered as he lowered his mouth to her neck.

She couldn't help the small laugh that escaped her. "You keep condoms in your wallet?"

"Just one," he said, rotating his hip against her. "I'm a guy. We're always hopeful when it comes to the idea of getting lucky and want to be prepared."

"Go get it," Heather said.

He pushed up to do as she ordered.

Since a bed was made up on the couch, she pushed off the pajama pants and then crawled under one of the blankets.

Martin took off the t-shirt to reveal a muscled chest. He pushed the sweatpants down on his hips just enough to free his arousal and put the condom on.

Heather lifted the blanket so he could crawl over her. His hand instantly pushed her cami up to free a

MICHELLE M. PILLOW

breast. His mouth claimed a nipple briefly. She lifted her hips in offering.

Martin didn't deny her. He drew his hips forward. The sweatpants clung to his thighs as she grabbed his naked ass. Being with a man was so much better than a silicone boyfriend. He entered her with a confident stroke.

Martin looked into her eyes as he moved inside her. Their breathing mingled, but otherwise they stayed quiet. His hips found a perfect rhythm, and he read her reactions. Pleasure built, and her climax came with an earth-shattering release. She tensed as it overtook her body.

Martin stiffened and jerked as he found his climax. His hips flexed, and he kept himself tight against her. He breathed hard.

"Fuck," he whispered, and he somehow made the word sound like the best compliment she'd ever received.

Heather smiled, trying to catch her breath. Her heart beat fast, and she waited for it to slow.

Martin sat back and reached for a tissue to wrap the condom. He pulled his pants to cover his hips.

Heather tugged down her cami. He touched her thigh, keeping her from putting on the pajama pants as he looked at her.

"You're so beautiful," he said, his voice soft.

"So are you," she answered.

"I want you to know I don't take this lightly. I don't want this to be a one-time thing." His eyes roamed over her. "I *definitely* do not want this to be a one-time thing."

"Me either." Heather wasn't sure she could move. Sex had released her tension, but the relaxation combined with her exhaustion caused her eyelids to blink heavily.

Martin stood and went to throw the condom away.

Heather forced herself to pull on her pants and sit up. When he returned, she said, "I should go sleep in Viv's room so no one discovers us out here but know I don't want to leave you."

"I don't want you to go either," he said, sitting beside her. He kissed the corner of her mouth. "Before you go, I want to ask you out on a proper date. I'll take you to that new fancy restaurant downtown, treat you like you deserve."

"That steakhouse?" Heather asked, shaking her head. She covered her mouth as she yawned. "No, they serve the fancy cake."

"Fancy cake?" Martin arched a brow. "What's that?"

"You know, fancy cake. When you eat at a nice restaurant and order dessert and the cake sliver that they give you is one-sixteenth of an inch thick and ridiculously tiny, but you can't order twelve of them to make a normal size piece because they'll shame you like you're a glutton."

"Ah. Fancy cake." He nodded.

"Cake is the most important meal of the day," she said, only half-serious.

He chuckled. "I'll keep that in mind. So yes to the date, no to the steakhouse, yes to the grocery store bakery for a non-fancy real cake we eat in the parking lot in my truck?"

"Yes," she said. "You do know how to charm a woman."

Martin chuckled.

Heather leaned to kiss him softly. "I'll see you in the morning."

"Good night, Heather, sweet dreams." Martin looked like he wanted to beg her to stay with him. They both knew that wasn't possible.

Heather stood and forced her legs to carry her down the hall. For a crappy day, it hadn't ended badly at all.

CHAPTER FIFTEEN

HEATHER WANTED to stop and breathe, but life wouldn't let her. It started with the phone, which rang more than Muffy pulling a prank. First, her mother called bright and early the next morning to check on her. Then, her mother called an hour later to ask something about casserole preferences. Then, an hour after that to check on her. And, still, and hour after that for a progress update on the casseroles, and on and on it went.

Then there were the conversations with her insurance agent, the mortgage company, her tax accountant because half her receipts were burnt up, the police department, the fire department, numerous tenants calling to check on her and get the details, and the local paper. There was even a prerecorded spam message warning her that the warranty on her car was about to expire because why not?

The one call she didn't get was from Martin, and he was the only person she wanted to hear from.

There had been no time to talk with him the morning after the fire. He did smile at her, but a rush of conversation had surrounded them. Vivien had wanted everyone to get their stories straight. Lorna made sure everyone ate breakfast and lunch and snacks. Troy kept refilling her coffee for her and offering to help however she needed. Martin had been preoccupied with his daughter, going from needing to punish her to wanting to hug her. William's only goal seemed to be trying to make Heather laugh and keeping her calm.

As trying as they could sometimes be, she would not have been able to get through it without her family and friends.

There had been many questions about how the fire started.

Did she have enemies?

Did she have money problems?

Did she gamble?

Were disgruntled tenants recently evicted?

Why was she running a space heater this time of year?

Heather could tell they weren't entirely buying her story, but they could find no reason as to why she'd torch her own place when there were more valuable properties on her roster. It was only mildly disconcerting that Vivien ended up having a knack for lying to authorities, though not surprising when considering the number of times she'd talked her way out of trouble when they were children.

In the end, she was pretty sure it was her family's deep ties to the community that ended the investigation. She wasn't sure how to feel about that, but the other option was to get Jan into trouble for something Heather's son's spirit had convinced her to do. There was absolutely no way to tell that story.

Four tense days passed in a blur before the fire department finally cleared the property so she could have a crew board it up to keep animals and people from exploring inside. William volunteered to oversee the efforts for her. What little could be saved after the smoke damage she had delivered to her second storage unit. The structure wasn't worth saving, from a practical standpoint. Sentimentally, though, Heather wanted to hold on to it.

On top of all the practical and legal matters on Heather's mind, Muffy decided to call in her marker for Heather's help. Only, it turned out the only kind of help Muffy needed was someone to actively listen to her for hours at a time. The incessant talking caused Heather's eye to twitch, but as long as she nodded and glanced in Muffy's direction every once in a while, the spirit seemed content. Heather, on the other hand, had a throbbing headache.

When Heather pulled up to what remained of her home to check on the clean up progress, she saw Jan sitting on top of the wheel well in the back of her father's truck. The girl lifted her eyes as Heather parked her car only to drop them back down quickly.

"And he was like, you totally look hot, and I was like, I know I do." Muffy laughed. Heather nodded her head and forced a smile.

"Well, we're here," Heather said. "I'm sorry to have to cut this short but—"

Muffy disappeared.

"Never mind," she muttered as she got out of the vehicle.

Heather waved at a few of the men carrying plywood toward the backyard. She recognized them from her brother's work crew. Their hands were full so they only nodded in return.

Heather stopped near Martin's truck. "Hey, Jan."

"Hi." The tiny sound barely made it out of Jan's

mouth. She glanced at the house and then back down again.

"Have the others been talking to you?" Heather asked.

Jan tucked her chin tighter against her chest.

"You know you can talk about this with me," Heather insisted.

Jan didn't move.

Heather sighed. "Is your dad inside?"

Jan nodded.

Heather took a step toward the house.

"I'm sorry about your house," Jan said.

Heather stopped and went back to the truck. "Thank you for the apology. I know it's not always easy to admit when we do something wrong."

"I don't like Muffy. She talks *all the time*." Jan glanced up as if testing the conversation about ghosts.

Heather chuckled and nodded. "She does."

"I tell her to go away," Jan said.

"Does that work?"

"Sometimes." Jan stood up from the wheel well and crossed the bed of the truck to stand closer to Heather.

"I can help you with that." Heather lowered her voice and leaned against the truck. She rested her arms along the side. "My grandma told me that whenever I needed them to leave me alone to imagine that they're air. Look through them to something on the other side. It doesn't matter at what. It could be a tree or a wall or whatever, but you look at that tree like it's the most interesting tree you have ever seen. Then you look away and pretend like you can't hear them. The more you practice, the faster it will work."

"Do you think it would work so I can go to school?" she asked.

"Is that something you want?" Heather reached to push a strand of hair from Jan's face and tucked it behind her ear. At the contact, she felt the girl's insecurity.

She nodded.

"Then we'll practice and see if we can't make that happen," Heather said.

Jan smiled.

Heather ran her hand along her hair. "You are so pretty. Do you know who's excellent at styling hair? Viv. I bet she'd love to get her hands on your head at the next slumber party."

Jan's smile widened. "We can do that?"

"Try to stop us." Heather winked.

Heather looked at the sad remains of her home. Martin appeared from the backyard, looking like he checked on Jan. Seeing her, he lifted his hand and waved, but didn't return to what he'd been doing.

"He said it would help you," Jan said, not seeing her father watching them.

"Who, sweetie? Trav?" Heather felt her stomach tighten.

"He said you couldn't live in that house anymore or you'll become a ghost like him. He says you cry all the time in there." Jan patted Heather's hair, mimicking Heather's earlier gesture. "It's okay. I sometimes cry too. It's not nice. He said if we took away the house, then you couldn't look at his door and cry anymore."

Tears filled her eyes. "Does he talk to you a lot?"

"Sometimes," Jan said. "Sometimes we play games."

"Like tic-tac-toe at Anderson House?" Heather remembered the circle being drawn in the dust.

"No. That's Yancy. He's old. He takes his teeth out sometimes to make me laugh. He says the game is called noughts and crosses."

"Jan?" Martin called. "Are you being good?"

"Yes!" Jan yelled, turning to look at her father.

Heather wanted to know more about her son. She tried not to sound too eager or pushy, but she really wanted to grab Jan by the shoulders and make

249

her tell every single detail of the encounters. "What kind of games do you and Trav play?"

Jan shrugged. "Hide-and-seek, but it's not fair. He can always find me too fast. Sometimes we draw pictures. He gets mad when I ride my bike."

"Oh?" The sound was a little too high-pitched as Heather choked back the urge to sob. Did her son remember how he died? She thought of the mangled bike.

Martin must have seen her look because he hurried forward. "Jan, what did you say?"

Heather lifted her hand to stop him from scolding her. "No, she's fine. We're just talking."

Martin hesitated before nodding and backing away.

"Did he tell you why he's here?" Heather had hoped he'd moved on to a better place, and that is why she'd never seen him.

"No." Jan combed her fingers in Heather's hair. She lifted a lock from her shoulder and tried to braid a few of the strands.

"Can you see him now?" Heather asked.

Jan dropped Heather's hair and moved around the truck bed, looking over the yard. "No, but he might be playing hide-and-seek."

"Do you think he'd talk to me if we could find

him?" Heather felt as if she couldn't catch her breath. Her hands shook with the idea of seeing his face just one more time. "I want to talk to him."

"But you'll be sad," Jan objected.

"It's okay to be sad when you miss someone," Heather answered. "Please, I need to tell him something important. I need to talk to him. Please, will you find him and tell him?"

Jan looked over Heather's shoulder.

"Mom." The word came from behind. The voice had a mature quality to it, but how could a mother not recognize the sound of her child?

Heather's legs gave out, and she had to hold on to the truck to keep from falling. She turned toward the voice.

Trav stood in his striped shirt and ripped jeans. His brown hair was spiked with gel. He had been so particular about it.

Her hand slipped, and she dropped to the ground by the truck tire.

"Baby?" she whispered. "It's you. I've been looking for you everywhere."

She lifted her arms, wanting to hold him.

"Mom." He came to her. So much could be heard in that one perfect word. This time he sounded like a lost child.

Heather couldn't feel his solid form, but as the cold chill pushed against her, she felt him. She held her arms in front of her, able to remember what it felt like to hug him. She never wanted to let him go.

"I love you so much." Heather didn't stop her tears. "I've thought about you every day. I have loved you every single day. I miss you so much, sweet boy."

"Mom." This time the word was resolved. Trav pulled back, and she couldn't force him to stay next to her. "It's all right."

"Why haven't you shown yourself before now?" She couldn't look away, afraid that if she did, he would disappear.

His eyes went to Jan, and he smiled. "Hey, January."

"Hey," Jan answered.

"Trav, why did you burn down your room?" she asked.

"Because it makes you upset," he answered. "Now you can't stare at it and cry anymore. I don't want you to be sad anymore."

"Honey, I'm not sad because of a house. I'm sad because I miss you." She lifted her hand to let it hover next to his cheek. Her fingers tingled. "I'm so sorry that bad thing happened to you. I'm sorry that I couldn't protect you."

"You have to stop blaming yourself." He swayed on his feet. "You used to laugh all the time. I just want you to be happy. Grandpa Joe said seeing me would only make you sad longer. He said when he died that he visited Grandma Julia, but then she never moved on and was always a little sad."

"You see Grandpa Joe?" Heather asked. Joe had been Julia's husband. He'd moved on to the next step. Julia never precisely explained what the next step was. She said some mysteries had to be discovered at the right moment, but that it was beautiful.

"He said he'll teach me to play baseball when I go with him. He said we could play all the time, and climb giant trees, and that there are other kids there," the boyish excitement dropped into worry, "but I don't want you to be by yourself."

"That sounds so nice, baby," she assured him.

He sounded so excited by the prospect. Knowing he wouldn't be alone made her feel better. It wasn't the same as him being with her where he belonged. It wasn't fair. He deserved all the things a person experienced in life. But that's not what fate had in mind for him. Trav would never grow up and give her grandkids. He'd never have a job or find a wife.

Being a parent wasn't about what she wanted. It wasn't about her broken heart. A good mother sacrificed. That is what she had to do. She needed to put her son before herself.

"You should go with Grandpa Joe." Oh, but she didn't want to let him go.

"I have to make sure you're all right first," Travis said.

"I will be." She heard Jan move behind her, but still couldn't look away. She needed to take in every second.

Travis looked at his friend. "January doesn't have a mom."

Heather nodded.

"And you're a really good mom," he continued. He walked so that she was forced to turn toward the truck where she could see both children. "She said her dad worries all the time. Maybe if you were her mom, he wouldn't worry so much. And you wouldn't be lonely and sad because you'd have a kid to take care of."

Jan stared at Travis.

"Oh, Trav, those things are complicated," Heather answered.

"Don't be mad at her about the fire. I made her promise," he said.

"I'm not mad at her about the fire," Heather said.

"I mean, the fire was not a good thing, but I'm not mad. It just can't ever happen again."

"She's really good at drawing," he insisted. "And she's super funny."

Jan finally glanced over and tried to smile.

Heather realized that they were trying to sell her on the idea of taking care of the girl.

"Yes, January is an amazing girl," Heather agreed.

"So if you marry her dad, you can be her mom," Travis concluded. "And you don't have a house now, so you can live with them."

"Well..." Heather tried to think of how to explain the complications of adult romance and marriage to a couple of ten-year-olds. They had obviously thought their plan out.

"Don't you want to be a mom?" Travis insisted.

"Being a mom is the best thing in my entire life," Heather assured him. "And I would be honored to have a daughter as lovely as January, but things like marriage and living together are something that adults need to decide amongst themselves. It's very complicated."

The kids' expressions fell.

"But for now I can be like a mom, maybe?"

Heather offered. "I can be a friend, if January will have me?"

January smiled and nodded.

"See, I told you she was the best," Travis said to his friend.

Heather held out her arms. Both Jan and Travis came to her. She hugged Jan tight while feeling her son's energy.

"I love you, Mom," Travis whispered. His image began to fade as if he were losing the energy he needed to manifest. "Grandpa Joe says someday you will come where we are."

"I promise," Heather answered. "I can't wait."

"Can you send me to him?" Travis asked.

Heather nodded. "Be sure to tell Grandpa hi for me."

"I will." He grinned at Jan. "See you later, alligator."

"After a while, crocodile," she answered.

Travis chuckled.

"I love you so much," she said. "Forever and ever. I will think about you every day until we're together."

"I love you too, Mom." He continued to fade.

"Spirit, you have been found pure," Heather whispered the words from the séance book used to send a spirit to where they belonged. The words caught in her throat, and she had to take a deep breath before finishing, "I release you into the light. Go in peace and love."

Travis smiled. His spirit lifted like tiny beautiful embers floating up into the sky. Heather held Jan close as they watched him leave.

"I hate that he has to go," Jan said.

"Me too," Heather answered.

"Was that...?" Martin approached slowly. He glanced up to where they looked. "Did something happen?"

"Jan helped me say goodbye to my son," Heather said, not letting the girl go.

"He went to play baseball with his grandpa," Jan added. She pushed at Heather's arm to be released. When she stepped away, she said matter-of-factly, "I'm going to be over here. You two have a lot of grown-up stuff to talk about before Heather can move in with us."

Martin looked stunned as his daughter walked along the curb toward the neighbor's house with the boxer.

"You're moving in?" he asked.

Heather wiped the residual tears from her eyes. She would always miss him but knowing her sweet boy had moved on and was with family helped her heal more than she ever imagined possible.

"I thought maybe you decided you didn't want to see me after, you know, that night at Vivien's." Martin leaned against the truck.

"What gave you that impression?" she asked.

"You never called." Martin's gaze dipped to her mouth as if he thought about kissing her.

"You didn't call me," she countered.

"You had a lot going on. I figured you'd call me when it was convenient for you," Martin said. "But then I thought maybe you considered it more and decided my life was too complicated."

Heather couldn't help but shake her head. Out of the two of them, she wouldn't have said he was the more complicated.

"I wanted you to call," she said.

"I wanted you to call," he answered

"Well aren't we just a couple of teenagers?" Heather glanced up to the sky and then back again. "Our kids have it in their heads we belong together. They thought burning the house would make me move in with you and be Jan's mom."

Martin opened his mouth, but no sound came out.

"Don't worry. I'm not fishing for a proposal,"

Heather said. She came closer to him. "But maybe we start with a date in a grocery store parking lot and see where things go from there."

"No fancy cake," he said. "I think that can be arranged."

Martin cupped her cheek and gazed into her eyes. "Have I told you how amazing you are?"

Heather lifted on her toes. "Are you going to kiss me or what?"

Martin obeyed her request, leaning his mouth to capture hers. Her arms slid around his neck.

"*Ewww*," Jan yelled with a giggle. "That's grody to the max."

Martin pulled back. "Grody...? Where did she learn...?"

"Don't ask." Heather pulled him back against her. The hard rock of emotions in her chest dissipated, and she felt like she could breathe for the first time in over a decade. "Just keep kissing me."

Martin grinned and did just that.

CHAPTER SIXTEEN
EPILOGUE

FIVE MONTHS LATER...

Heather stared up at the half-painted siding of Old Anderson House. The crew was nearly finished with the exterior. The sound of the moving vans reverberated down the street. They'd finally dropped off the last load of boxes.

"I can't believe we're finally moved in," Vivien said from the doorway. "I mean, except for like fifty billion boxes to unpack, but we did it."

Heather grinned. Happiness filled her. Anderson House felt like a new beginning. She had a great relationship with Martin. Jan was starting public school soon. And her two best friends in the entire world were going to live with her in their favorite house.

There had been some talk of Martin, Troy, and

William also moving in, but they were going to see how things went. That was a lot of adults under the same roof. For now, this was precisely what Heather, Vivien, and Lorna needed.

"Who's hungry?" Lorna appeared next to Vivien. "January and I made a pork roast with a green pepper jelly glaze, lemon and parmesan asparagus, cheesy mashed potatoes, homemade dinner rolls, and chocolate cake. She's finishing setting the table now." She glanced around. "Where are the guys?"

"Liquor run," Heather said. "Not a house-warming feast without wine."

Vivien smirked and said softly so Jan couldn't overhear, "Condom run. Not a housewarming without—"

"You're awful," Lorna teased, swatting her with the hand towel she held. "Come help me finish up in the kitchen."

Vivien disappeared with Lorna inside.

Heather resumed looking at the siding. The sound of a car came from down the street, and she turned to watch William park next to the curb. Troy hopped out of the backseat carrying a bag. The sounds of clanking bottles revealed some of what was inside.

"They're almost ready in there," Heather said.

William grinned and patted his stomach as if anticipating the meal.

Martin climbed out of the passenger seat holding flowers. He smiled as he came to greet her. "Hey there sexy woman."

"Hey there sexy man," she answered with a laugh.

He handed her the bouquet and gave her a quick kiss. "Congratulations on the new home."

"Thank you." Heather smelled the flowers and smiled at the sweet gesture.

"Get in here, or we're not waiting," William yelled.

"Coming?" Martin asked.

"I'll be right there." Heather watched him go inside.

The sun had begun to set, streaking magentas and purples in the sky. She studied the roof against the clouds, content to just be. There was no list she needed to look at, no desperate need to fill the moment with anything but calm.

"I wish you could have been here for this, sweet boy," she whispered, "but I know we'll be together someday."

The sound of laughter came through the open front door. Heather moved to go inside.

"Excuse me?"

Heather turned at the sound. A redheaded woman stood holding a small box. Dark circles had formed under her eyes as if she hadn't slept for days.

"I know this is going to sound strange, but..." The woman stepped closer. "I think I'm supposed to be here. I think I'm meant to talk to you. I keep receiving signs that all point to this house."

"I'm sorry?" Heather asked, confused. She had no clue who the woman was or why she thought she should visit.

"Heather?" Vivien appeared at the doorway, sounding concerned. "What is it?"

The redhead pulled open the box and took out a ring. She held it between her shaking fingers. "Does this mean anything to you? Because when I touch it, I feel like I have to be here."

Heather glanced at the ring on her forefinger as her magic began to tingle. Lorna appeared next to Vivien. The two women came forward to join them on the lawn.

"You think I'm nuts, don't you?" She dropped the ring in the box and closed the lid. "I'm sorry for bothering you."

"No, wait," Vivien said. She shared a look with

Heather and Lorna. Something magical was happening here, and they all knew it.

"Are you hungry?" Lorna offered. "We're just about to have dinner."

"Yes, please come in and sit down," Heather said. The woman looked like she was about to fall over from exhaustion. "I think maybe this is where you're supposed to be."

Lorna hooked her arm around the woman's shoulders and led her inside.

Vivien fell into step next to Heather. "What's Julia up to now?"

"I don't know, but it can't be a coincidence that she shows up today of all days when we are moving into our new home. Plus, she has one of Julia's rings," Heather answered. "I guess there is only one way to find out."

Vivien gave Heather's back a small pat and chuckled as they went into the house. Vivien shut the door and said, "Here we go again."

The End

THE FIFTH SENSE
ORDER OF MAGIC BOOK 4

The Series Continues

Some secrets refuse to stay buried.

By all rights, Sue Jewel should be dead. Instead of celebrating her fortieth birthday, she was wrapped in plastic and stuffed in the trunk of a car. Worst part is the man she promised to spend her life with is the one who tried to kill her. With a little help from Fate, Sue walks away from the ordeal, but her husband doesn't.

Now with a new lease on life, Sue wants to put as much mileage between her past and her present as she can. It would be a lot easier if something supernatural with dark intent wasn't along for the ride. Desperate to break free from it all, she finds herself in Freewild Cove, making new friends, catching the eye of the handsome coffee shop owner, and hoping to magically cut her ties to her would-be murderer once and for all.

Lorna, Vivien, and Heather are back. And with the help of Grandma Julia's ghost, they're kicking supernatural butt and taking names!

Order of Magic 4: The Fifth Sense

SECOND CHANCE MAGIC
ORDER OF MAGIC BOOK 1

Secrets broke her heart... and have now come back
from the grave to haunt her.

So far, Lorna Addams' forties are not what she
expected. After a very public embarrassment, she
finds it difficult to trust her judgment when it comes
to new friendships and dating. She might be willing
to give love a second chance when she meets the
attractive William Warrick, if only she could come to
terms with what her husband did to her and leave it
in the past.

How is a humiliated empty nest widow supposed
to move on with her life? It's not like she can develop
a sixth sense, séance her ex back, force him to tell her
why and give her closure. Or can she?

THIRD TIME'S A CHARM
ORDER OF MAGIC BOOK 2

Friends don't let friends séance drunk.

Vivien Stone lost the love of her life over twenty years ago. Now that she's in her forties with a string of meaningless relationships under her belt, she can't help but pine for what might have been. It doesn't help that she's somewhat psychic and can pretty much predict where a relationship is heading before it even starts.

When she and her best friends find a hidden book of séances, Vivien believes it's the perfect opportunity to talk to her lost love. But things don't go as planned and what was meant to be a romantic reunion takes a turn for the bizarre.

Maybe some things (and people) are better left

buried in the past, and what she really needs has
been standing in front of her all along.

NEWSLETTER

To stay informed about when a new book in the series installments is released, sign up for updates:

Sign up for Michelle's Newsletter

michellepillow.com/author-updates

ABOUT MICHELLE M. PILLOW

New York Times & *USA TODAY* Bestselling Author

Michelle loves to travel and try new things, whether it's a paranormal investigation of an old Vaudeville Theatre or climbing Mayan temples in Belize. She believes life is an adventure fueled by copious amounts of coffee.

Newly relocated to the American South, Michelle is involved in various film and documentary projects with her talented director husband. She is mom to a fantastic artist. And she's managed by a dog and cat who make sure she's meeting her deadlines.

For the most part she can be found wearing pajama pants and working in her office. There may or may not be dancing. It's all part of the creative process.

Come say hello! Michelle loves talking with readers on social media!

www.MichellePillow.com

facebook.com/AuthorMichellePillow

twitter.com/michellepillow

instagram.com/michellempillow

bookbub.com/authors/michelle-m-pillow

goodreads.com/Michelle_Pillow

amazon.com/author/michellepillow

youtube.com/michellepillow

pinterest.com/michellepillow

COMPLIMENTARY MATERIAL

SPELLBOUND
WARLOCKS MACGREGOR® BOOK 2

Let Sleeping Warlocks Lie...

Iain MacGregor knows how his warlock family feels about outsiders discovering the truth of their powers, its forbidden. That doesn't seem to stop him from having accidental magickal discharges whenever he's around the woman who has captured his attention. Apparently his magick and other "parts" don't seem to care what the rules are, or that the object of his affection just might be his undoing.

Warning: Contains yummy, hot, mischievous MacGregor boys who may or may not be wearing clothing and who are almost certainly up to no good on their quest to find true love.

WARLOCKS MACGREGOR® 2: SPELLBOUND: EXTENDED EXCERPT

"Dè tha thu ag iarraidh?"

"What do I want?" Jane whispered, looking around in confusion for the speaker. She was unsure as to how she'd come to be outside. One moment she'd been in bed, the next in a garden. "I'm losing my mind."

She knew this garden. She'd itched to get her hands on it ever since she'd moved to Green Vallis, Wisconsin. The plants were choking from neglect, but beneath their twisted wildness was rich soil. Most of the trees and shrubs would be salvageable—if not at their current location, then transplanted else-where. The grounds were expansive and had so much potential. Being located on a hill above the small town, it had ample sunlight and natural drainage when it rained. It belonged to an old mansion that had just recently been purchased after decades of sitting empty. Everyone in town knew the story of its builder—the displaced English lord. He'd been a rake or a rogue or whatever they called the rambunctiously decadent men of the time.

Despite whatever the nobleman had lacked in his personal life, he'd had a great eye for creating picturesque beauty. The property came with eighty acres of land, including part of the surrounding forest with a stream running through it and the old English landscape garden. Yes, the giant house was nice, but Jane saw it more as a backdrop to the nature surrounding it. She couldn't imagine owning eighty acres of land. The mere idea of it was a kind of what-would-you-do-if-you-won-a-million-dollars pipe dream.

"Dè tha thu ag iarraidh!"

Jane flinched as she found the bearer of the mysterious voice. Why was a Scottish woman screaming at her? And why was the woman's tiny frame aging so rapidly Jane could see the wrinkles forming on the pretty face as if the woman was living an entire lifetime in a single afternoon?

Jane knew she was hallucinating. What else could this be? The doctors had warned her that her mind would eventually deteriorate. Even so, this hallucination felt very familiar as if she'd lived this moment but couldn't remember it.

"Thalla's cagainn bruis!"

"Chew a brush?" Jane tried to translate the woman's words. It made no logical sense that she understood any of it, as she didn't speak Gaelic. She frowned, looking at an overgrown gooseberry bush a few feet from where she stood on the cobblestone path. Not knowing why she tried to obey, she lifted her arm in its direction but couldn't reach. Why couldn't she reach it?

She looked down. A light fog surrounded her legs. It held her immobile like metal shackles. Fog like shackles? She should be able to run through the fog.

"*Dè tha thu ag iarraidh?*"

"I don't know what I want," Jane answered, blinking rapidly as a wrinkled finger pointed a little too close to her nose. How could the finger be so close? The woman was nearly twelve feet away down the path near the mansion's exterior wall. Fear filled her, nearly choking the breath from her lungs. "Why can I understand what you're saying? Who are you? How did I get here? What do you want?" She remained rooted in place, like the wild overgrowth around her yearning to be saved. "I don't understand why you're yelling at me."

The aging woman's finger dissipated into mist but did not disappear. Instead, the mist surrounded Jane's head. She swatted it away, but the action only caused the mist to swirl up her nose. Around her, the plants moved, coming to animated life. They stretched and grew, aging like the now-old woman before her, then transforming into a beautiful combination of lilac and purple Scottish heather. The heady scent of flowers and honey was so strong it burned her nostrils and caused her eyes to water. Bagpipes sounded in the distance, impossibly carried on a wind that did not stir.

And then...nothingness.

WARLOCKS MACGREGOR® SERIES

Love Potions
Spellbound
Stirring Up Trouble
Cauldrons and Confessions
Spirits and Spells
Kisses and Curses
Magick and Mischief
A Dash of Destiny

More Coming Soon

Visit www.MichellePillow.com for details.

PLEASE LEAVE A REVIEW
THANK YOU FOR READING!

Please take a moment to share your thoughts by reviewing this book.

Be sure to check out Michelle's other titles at www.MichellePillow.com

CPSIA information can be obtained
at www.ICGtesting.com
Printed in the USA
LVHW111039210821
695815LV00020B/448

9 781625 012517